Bridget was a different person in every way from the teenage girl who had loved Gareth Evans years ago and had her heart broken for her pains. Now, unexpectedly, she had met him again, and realised that even though she had changed, her love for him had not. But Gareth didn't even know her now . . .

HILLS OF AMETHYST

BY

MARY MOORE

MILLS & BOON LIMITED
15-16 BROOK'S MEWS
LONDON W1A 1DR

First published 1981
Australian copyright 1981
Philippine copyright 1981
This edition 1981

© Mary Moore 1981

ISBN 0 263 73552 4

Set in Monophoto Baskerville 11 on 11 pt.

Made and printed in Great Britain by
Richard Clay (The Chaucer Press) Ltd,
Bungay, Suffolk

CHAPTER ONE

BRIDGET MARLOW stood on the moonlit path, shivering slightly in spite of the heavy thick-knit cardigan she had put over her shoulders. Bother the girls who still chattered on in spite of her two previous warnings! She stood below the open-air dormitory, preparing to sear them with her wrath, when she heard her own name come floating down clearly on the still frosty night air.

'Bridget! Oh, Jody, you fool—who would want old Frigid Bridget trailing along behind? Imagine me asking Miss Frigidaire!'

There were hoots of ribald laughter from the other girls. Bridget did not need to ask who the speaker was. It was Valinda Mason, known to most of the staff as Valinda the Terrible. If there was trouble, mayhem or murder it just could not happen without the joyful stirring hand of Valinda. She made Bridget think of a Georgette Heyer heroine, with her close-cropped red curls, vivid blue eyes and fragile bone structure, a pocket-sized Venus. How someone who was so blessed with such beauty, brains and vitality, and a background of wealth could be such a tearaway was a puzzle.

Bridget hesitated for a moment. If Valinda had something planned for her, she preferred to know in advance. To be forewarned is to be forearmed.

Jody's voice was heavily sarcastic. 'You lot are all alike. I think Miss Marlow is super. You just make superficial judgments. You'd be surprised if you knew what I know about her.'

Bridget waited expectantly while Valinda jeered, 'Well, spill it out. Surprise me and tell me she's human, that red blood flows in her veins and that if she smiled her head wouldn't fall off. Go on, surprise me!'

Bridget grinned in the darkness. She had followed the Principal's very sound advice not to get too friendly with the girls. 'Laugh with them today, and they'll laugh at you tomorrow, I've seen it so often. You keep your distance and you may be able to keep them in line. I'm warning you.'

And Valinda was the worst of the bunch. Many a housemistress had met her Waterloo at the hands of Valinda, and Bridget had no desire to make herself a sitting target.

The previous Matron had resigned when she found she had been outwitted by Valinda in an incredibly well thought out manoeuvre. Bridget had been appalled when she had heard the story and, while admitting that the Matron had got no more than she deserved, she had a healthy respect for Valinda's strategy. The Matron had apparently been reading Valinda's diary when she was at school, and became very adept at catching the rebel in her escapades, until Valinda carefully worked out the percentage of the times she was caught and lost privileges compared with the rest of the boarders. At first she thought she had a Judas in her dorm, but by some means which Bridget hated to dwell on she eliminated that theory, and one day returning to her room unexpectedly during school hours saw the Matron reading her private diary. From then on she wrote exactly what she wanted the Matron to read and let herself be caught often enough to allay suspicion.

Then she carefully built up an entirely fictitious romance with a boy boarder from the brother school. Week by week, the story became more lurid and more graphic in the description of their illicit meetings, wild orgies with drinks and drugs freely mixed.

The Matron stalked the pages of the diary as a lioness stalks her prey, and was at last rewarded with the cryptic note, 'Smithy between 12 and 2 a.m. Bot. Gard 200 yds due W. of totem pole 23rd.' It was no coincidence that the night chosen was the longest and predictably coldest night of the year, and the spot so far from the road that there was no chance the watchers could sit comfortably in a warm car to keep it under surveillance.

When the Principal and Matron returned in the early hours of the morning, both frozen almost as stiff as the totem pole, it was no wonder their tempers, already slightly frayed, were further stretched to find Valinda sound asleep looking incredibly innocent. The Principal firmly demanded proof of the impeccable source from which the Matron had made such wild allegations, and was definitely offended when the Matron had jerked open the top drawer of the dresser and handed her Valinda's diary.

Casting a withering glance at the infuriated Matron, she politely asked Valinda's permission to read the last week's entry and when it was granted, stoically read her way through the trivia that Valinda had written in a duplicate diary especially for the occasion.

The Matron left the following morning and Valinda's behaviour had been impeccable for several weeks.

Remembering this, Bridget determined to hear

what was planned for her, even if it took another half hour.

Jody was still energetically defending her judgment. 'I tell you, she's okay. And you do want a chaperon, and it is to go up in the mountains, so how many are you going to get volunteering? Plus the fact that you drive most people over twenty to an instant mental collapse. Now, from my acute observations, I *know* that any mention of the high country, musterers, mountains, is the only thing that gets her going. She goes all soft . . .'

'She *is* all soft.' Marsha's sharply critical tone was easily identified.

'No, she's not . . . she's deep frozen, frigid— probably hopelessly neurotic. I don't want to be stuck with her for six to eight weeks.'

'I'll second that,' Bridget muttered under her breath.

'Perhaps you could kid one of those mighty mountain men to rape her and she might thaw,' Marsha laughed spitefully. 'If they could find the body in that mess of clothes she goes round in.'

'Perhaps,' Valinda said thoughtfully, giving the idea careful consideration. 'No! She's too deep-frozen. Nothing would defrost her—not even the hottest breath in the West.'

'Who's he?' a chorus of eager voices gasped.

'As if I'd tell,' Valinda replied with crushing effect. 'Anyway, to expand on the overfrozen bit, Miss Frigidaire would be like a porterhouse steak that's been left too long in the freezer, the pallid flabby dead meat with all the blood drained into a separate pool. Yuck! How could I encourage *anybody* to make a pass at her, let alone *want* to rape her?'

'You're all wrong, and you're all *stupid*!' Jody's voice squeaked with impatience. 'If you saw her as she really is, it would blow your minds—your tiny minds. She is special ... very sexy. I meant to keep it a secret, but you're so bitchy I thought I'd let you know that you're all wrong. She's like ... like ... Wonder Woman. She can change ...'

Hoots of disbelieving hysterical laughter drowned Jody's voice.

'Does she wear striped underwear? How many motor cars have you seen her lift back on the road? Does she deflect bullets with her bare hands?'

When the voices died down Jody said quietly, 'Okay, I know that sounded silly, but she's dressed up in that creepy gear for some reason I don't know. I saw her one night and she looked super—slim as a reed, leggy, you know, high-breasted, tiny waist, neat bottom, and flat stomach, *and* her hair just floats straight and loose way past her shoulders. And she doesn't need glasses ... she has the most beautiful hazel eyes, greeny-gold, like the sunlight on the sea ...'

'Jody has a crush on the icicle ... Jody's ...'

'Shut up!' Valinda's voice curled like a whiplash and Bridget could almost feel the surprised silence. 'Go on, Jody.'

'Well, I know the glasses are fake because I handed her a poem of mine to read and she took them off to read it, and when she finished she turned to me and ... smiled, and I knew then that she was a real person behind that cover ... I can't describe it, but I was warmed by the intimacy of that moment. She has intelligence and depth ... you go on about being deep-frozen, that's not it ... More like a cool store—yes, she's put her emotions in a cool store, and marked them "Not to be used on the journey".'

Bridget shivered . . . that shy, wistful, dreamy Jody should show such perception was frightening.

'Go on,' Valinda ordered, and there was an alert quality in her tone which scared Bridget even more. You could almost hear her brain working like a computer, storing and rejecting Jody's impressions ready for future calculations. Bridget moved towards the stairs. It was like being dissected without an-aesthetic.

'A case of arrested development,' Jody continued with all the skill of a surgeon wielding a scalpel. 'Something mighty happened to her . . . an emotional experience that she couldn't handle, and she's closed up shop . . . not recently, it's not fresh, because her mask is part of her personality now, practised, controlled. She's more like a Sleeping Beauty. Talking to her I get the same feeling I get when I wake up at dawn and wait for the sunrise . . . there's a moment, a waiting, a hush, a stillness just before that moment of glory. I'm putting it badly, but it's tremendous. *Dynamite*.'

There was silence for a moment, then Valinda summed it up succinctly, 'Not an iceberg, but Mount Egmont, a snow-topped volcano. Interesting. You're rarely wrong about people, Jody.'

'Jody's in love . . . Jody's got a crush on Frigid Bridget,' Marsha jeered.

Bridget had had enough. She took the wide out-side fire escape two steps at a time. She threw the door of the dormitory wide open, and in a voice that was truly glacial announced, 'All girls in this dor-mitory have been warned twice already tonight, so as there's no hope of you taking any notice of a third warning we will dispense with it. None of you will attend the end-of-term dance next Friday night. However, you will be permitted to talk all that night without restriction instead. Now I want silence. Goodnight.'

Bridget was shaking as she made her way back to the Matron's flat. She was ashamed of having reacted so violently to Jody's probing of her character. But she felt like a tortoise with its shell ripped off. No child of sixteen should have the ability to see into a person's soul. She should have been warned when she heard the form mistress talking about the almost genius quality of Jody's essays, but she had been taken in by the soft gentle voice and unassuming air.

She let the water of the shower ease away some of her irrational irritability and used her body cologne with an abandoned hand. Banning them from the dance was a bit drastic . . . sort of overkill for talking after lights out. She grinned, her equilibrium restored. She just might relent, depending on their attitude tomorrow morning, but it would not hurt the little beasts to spend the night in suffering. Disappointment was a part of life, and suffering built character, or so the Bible said. And that lot could stand a fair bit of character building!

Her silk nightdress was lying on the bed and she walked towards it thoughtfully, then stopped in front of the full-length mirror, appraising and admiring the slender naked body reflected there. Jody had been right about those firm thrusting breasts and the long, lean flanks. Yes, she had a good body. There was no pride in her appraisal, just admiration and gratitude. Hard to believe that all her life she had been grossly overweight, stolid, unattractive, hating herself. Then when she was eighteen it had slid away unnoticed, leaving this elegant desirable shape. Fantastic. She would never get over the pleasure it gave her to see the metamorphosis. Some miracle— but too late.

She freed her hair and watched it tumble down like a shining honey-coloured curtain about her face and shoulders. Her hair was thick and lustrous, almost tawny in shade, like a field of ripened wheat, sometimes golden, sometimes dark, changing as the light touched it. Quickly she wove it into a single plait and examined her face objectively in the mirror. A good ordinary-looking face, oval in shape, neat nose, greeny-golden eyes with dark delicately arched eyebrows and long dark eyelashes, tipped with gold as was her hair. Not a raving beauty by any stretch of the imagination, but Bridget was perfectly content with what she saw. All her life up till three years ago she had avoided mirrors most carefully, hating the fat round plum-pudding face that had stared back at her, the eyes like currants imbedded in dough.

She turned her head, admiring the slender column of her neck and the firm youthful curve of her cheekline, then winked at her reflection. 'We've come a long way together, face, and you do me proud.' The image winked back in a conspiratorial fashion, and the smile widened attractively to reveal a deep, audacious dimple which altered the whole aspect of her face.

Bridget sighed, 'What a pity we didn't have this to offer Gareth four years ago.'

She switched out the light and snuggled down in her bed, hoping to drop off immediately, but sleep eluded her completely. Her mind kept going back to Jody's comments. Yes, it was true that she had stored her emotions out of harm's way after Gareth announced his engagement, but Jody was wrong about the sunrise aspect and the glory to come . . . the glory had been, and the stillness and quiet Jody had felt was like the world after sunset. There was nothing waiting in her life, no expectancy . . . because when you have tasted the ultimate, there is no chance of settling for second best.

But then Gareth had been special. For a moment his image was before her, with his thick shock of dark hair and his warm intelligent brown eyes and his slow easy smile revealing strong white teeth in a lean tanned face. Oh, he had been a charmer all right, tall and rangy, carrying himself with that arrogant assurance of the wealthy and well educated class . . . so sure of himself. And why shouldn't he be? Gareth had that rare ability to draw people to himself. Old ladies loved him, children adored him, and young ladies tried everything in the book to gain his attention. Men respected him. He was a natural leader, always getting the best out of those he worked with because he was prepared to give the best of himself to whatever work he was engaged in.

Bridget never had any trouble understanding why she had loved him, but she could never understand why he had bothered with her. Pity? Compassion? And yet it had been more than that. She only knew that she had never put herself forward, that he had singled her out from the start to be especially his.

How lonely she had been that summer she turned sixteen, fat beyond the description of plumpness, withdrawn into her studies at school, completely shattered by any social encounter outside the school routine, and most inside it. And her parents so far away. They were the only people she could relate

to, and even then she had wondered what strange
fate had given such wonderful parents such a weird
offspring. Her father had been such a handsome,
loving man, and her mother small, dainty and
beautiful. Bridget had always cringed at the astonishment people displayed when she was introduced.
This is your daughter? It didn't help.

But they were in South America for those two
years and Mr and Mrs Deveraux who owned the
beautiful high country station had, in their kindness
and respect for the missionary work they were
engaged in, volunteered to take Bridget for the long
summer vacation . . . and Gareth had been working
there, living in the house. So she had seen him every
day, those long lovely summer days of December and
January, when she had been sixteen. The next year
they invited her back, and she had gone, just to be
near him, to see him each day. *Oh, Gareth!*

She turned restlessly in her bed. What had made
that wonderful man choose such a fat, frumpy, ugly,
awkward girl for his close companion? He had been
twenty-two, the star attraction wherever he was, yet
from the first evening she had arrived he had
adopted her. The wonder of it was with her yet. He
had coaxed her, teased her, bullied her, until she
went with him most days in his Landrover, or on his
motorbike, or just was near him at the sheep yards,
or at the cattle yards. And when he was not working
he made it obvious to all that she, Bridget, was his
choice to sit with in the evenings, to partner him to
dances or barbecues, or to go in his jet boat, or to
swim with him.

The station people had at first been vastly amused,
then grew to accept it totally. But she had never
learned to accept it totally. Each time Gareth kept

her a place by him in the car, or came searching for her at a party, each time she met the warm laughing intimacy of his brown eyes or shared a confidence with him, the experience was as new and as fresh as the first time.

When he had reached out his hand to help her out of the boat, or flung his arm about her to give her a hug as a welcome after he'd been out somewhere she couldn't go, her whole heart had been filled with awe and love and gratitude, and she knew that heaven itself had no greater joy to offer her than the joy of being with Gareth.

Had he just been using her for protection against the predatory females, who saw in him a more than eligible bachelor? He was the son of an extremely wealthy landowner up in the North Island, destined to share in the control of a huge farming complex with his father and brother when he had gained valuable experience on some of the South Island stations. He was handsome, he was charming and he was definitely unavailable . . . because of her. And yet she knew he liked her. They shared so much as they grew to know each other. They had flowed together as two tributaries meeting from different valleys flow into a river. Thoughts, ideas, fears and secret deep-down desires formed a fabric of friendship that had the feeling of indestructibility.

And on her seventeenth birthday, the day before she left the station, he had walked with her in the moonlight, and under a canopy of stars, with the mountain air sweet and warm like summer wine, he had kissed her. It was not a light kiss as a friend gives another friend on their birthday, but a kiss that exploded her whole world, and there was the glory that Jody had seen. Gareth kissed her again at the door, and again the glory, the flowing between them of love so strong and powerful, so deep and true that the pain and joy were indistinguishable . . . a pleading and a promise, a giving and a receiving, a question and an answer that needed no words.

Had it only been in her imagination? Angrily Bridget found tears on her face and leaned round to find a tissue. Why, it was years since she had cried for Gareth. Years and years and years. Calf love? Schoolgirl crush? It might have been, until that kiss, and then it had been real man–woman love. She had changed that night from a child to a woman and had no desire to go back to innocence. And she had never seen him again, and would never see him again, but he had spoiled her for ever choosing anyone else.

She had joined her parents in England and gone to university there for two years, shaking the dust of New Zealand from her sturdy brogues without a backward glance, after she had had a note from Mrs Deveraux telling of Gareth's engagement to a friend from up North, a sweet girl who had grown up next door to him. The family were delighted.

By the time her eighteenth birthday arrived she had got over most of the pain of losing Gareth and her beautiful dream world, but she had suffered, and the scar tissue was easily disturbed. Her parents had been fantastic, loving her throughout her most fierce times of sorrow, of grief, of resentment and anger, and they loved her still. Not a bad track record, considering how she emerged from the battle—aggressive and acquiring a very nasty turn of phrase as a defence mechanism.

She had been completely unaware of the dramatic changes in her shape, apart from noticing that she was thinner, a little, until Andrew had told her she was beautiful. How she had laughed that night! It was the funniest thing she had ever heard, and of course she didn't believe him. When you have known all your life that you're ugly, it takes more than losing a few pounds to convince you that you're not Dracula. But other men besides Andrew had started to ask her out and begun to flatter her with their attention, and she scornfully demolished them with a vixen tongue and a well balanced chip on each shoulder. It made no difference. In fact, her total rejection of the male population of her particular varsity set only seemed to encourage them, like the challenge of an unstormable citadel.

She returned for her second year to find that, through no fault of her own, she was a very much sought after girl, with both the girls and men of her class, and decided to join their foolishness instead of standing back whipping them with her withering scorn. She threw herself into the party scene with a feverishness that had a touch of madness. It lasted for more time than she cared to remember, then one night in a smoke-filled, dimly lit flat among the drunk and very drunk leftovers from a weekend of excesses she came to her senses.

She had picked up her coat and bag and left with utter thankfulness. She had not been enjoying herself, it was not her style, and she had been senselessly searching to find another Gareth, someone to fill the emptiness in her heart, trying to prove the unprovable. The only men she ever dated were those who had something of Gareth in their make-up, the dark hair or brown eyes, even a voice that held an echo of his . . . How stupid she had been! There was no one like Gareth, there never would be, and he could never be hers, and no substitute would do.

She had dropped out of university, cut herself off from the old crowd and taken a course in child care, doing the practical work at a nearby hospital. Gradually, over the following months, the wildness in her nature softened, and as she daily came in contact with the young children in the terminal cancer ward something of their courage and acceptance of life became hers, so that she gained a peace and a steadiness that was beyond value. She would have been there still if it had not been for Andrew.

Angrily, Bridget threw back the blankets and snatched up her robe. There was no sleep in her bed tonight. She switched on the electric jug and made herself an evilly strong cup of coffee, snatched up a book. Damn Jody for setting these long-forgotten memories swirling in her mind! No, that was not fair. She herself was to blame, for returning to New Zealand. She had been weak and stupid to think it would make any difference to her outlook on life just to return to the country where she had known such happiness.

She didn't want to see Gareth again. She was no longer in love with him. Sure, she loved him still, but that was because she had worked so terribly hard at hating him, and failed. He just remained in her heart as a very dear and precious memory. He was married, permanently removed from her life, and she accepted that completely. But what lingered still, indelibly etched in her mind, was how she had felt when she was in love with him and the knowledge that no other man could lift her to that same height of ecstasy and awareness. The rapture, the joy of being in his presence, the feeling that at last she knew what she had been created for, a knowledge that way back in the mist of the beginning of time God had ordained them for each other, was the single insurmountable barrier that kept her from forming any deep relationship with any other man.

She had come to terms with it, accepted it, not angrily or resentfully, but calmly and intelligently. Life had plenty to offer besides marriage. If she could accept, why couldn't Andrew? Why couldn't her parents? Why had they encouraged, almost forced her into a return visit to New Zealand? It was a complete waste of money, she had known that before she left England, and each day here reinforced her belief. It wasn't the country, beautiful as it was, that held her heart. And it was *her* money that they were wasting so frivolously . . . they were so stupid. It was her only money, a two-thousand-pound legacy from her grandmother, that they had made her spend in such a wanton, wasteful manner.

Wearily she pushed aside her book. It was all Andrew's fault. When she had dropped out of varsity life her former friends had forgotten her completely, all except Andrew. He had searched for her, and tracked her down and in spite of her firm rejection of him, had persisted until he had become established as a friend. And that was all he would ever be . . . but he just would not believe it. He wanted to marry her, but she had nothing to offer . . . just friendship.

'Go back to New Zealand and have a look at Gareth. You've built him up to some sort of a superman, and he's just as human as the rest of us. He's nothing special. He'll have a couple of kids by now, and just see how romantic he looks wearing the typical harassed look of a subdued husband, changing the kids' dirty nappies, wiping their unattractive runny noses.'

And Bridget had laughed, 'Oh, Andrew, for an intelligent man you're awfully stupid. You're a doctor, Dr Andrew Kiloran, handsome, suave, witty, and well established—you could have any girl. You only want me because you can't have me. It's an ego thing. And anyway, Gareth was fantastic with kids, he'd make a marvellous father.'

Andrew had remained unruffled. 'Go and see him. The sight of you should blight the rest of his life. I don't see why I should be the only one to suffer.'

'He wouldn't even know me. You know Mother and Father's friends never recognise me from the kid I was . . . a true ugly duckling story. Although I prefer Mother's version of a chrysalis shedding its shell to let the butterfly emerge. Why, even my name was different. He knew me as Bonnie, a nickname I grew up with, but got rid of when I came back to England. I guarantee I could be introduced to him, and he'd not remember me.'

'Go and see him, anyway. I'm convinced that having seen him, you'll come back and find me irresistible. Most girls do. Show him the new you.'

Bridget had giggled. 'Go over and say, "Ya! Ya! See what you missed!" '

Andrew had not smiled. 'That's exactly what I mean. One look at you and your cornsilk hair and that gorgeous body ripe and waiting for a man to pleasure it should bring such a light to his eyes and such a regret to his heart that you'll walk away smiling . . . and he'll be forgotten for ever.'

When Bridget had shared Andrew's idea with her parents, expecting them to laugh with her, she had been surprised that they had approved of his ridiculous idea. At first she had been hurt by their lack of understanding, then angry, and then finally wearied by their combined arguments, had given in and bought her ticket, not even understanding her own motives.

She had determined to arrive, get herself a job, stay six months, not see or contact Gareth, and return home showing them the silliness of their plans. It had not been easy to get work, and only by donning the ridiculous garb and glasses had she been able to appear old enough to take on the temporary position of Matron of this girls' school. It had been fun in a way, but she would have to start looking for other work or return home.

Actually, coming to New Zealand had solved nothing, indeed had only made the situation more complex. She had been here three months and had made no attempt to search Gareth out. She had no intention of doing so, as his world was no longer hers and could never be, and she knew that to meet him would carry no special significance, for her or for him ... four years was a long time. They would meet, and greet each other, a little awkwardly at first, then reminisce and go their separate ways. The complication was the fact that being thousands of miles away from Andrew had confirmed the fact that she had no particular feeling for him at all, no sense of longing to rush back and be with him. She enjoyed his letters, but if they failed to arrive with their accustomed regularity she did not panic or feel anxious that he might have found someone more interesting. In fact she always searched his letters hopefully for such news.

She had tried to put this exact point to him before she left, and had all her well-reasoned arguments swept aside with his succinct and confident retort of 'Rubbish!' Bridget hated to hurt him, but she had no intention of marrying him just because she did not want to disappoint him. Oh, she did wish people would keep out of her life and let her get on with living it! There was much more to life than men and marriage, and from what she saw in the lives of her own age group, marriage was a fairly dicey proposition. Sure, at one time she had thought that being a wife, having children to love and care for, was the very essence of life, but now she was content—no, delighted to settle for being captain of her own ship. It was by far the easiest way.

As for love, there were plenty of unloved children in the world, plenty of hurt and bewildered people who needed affection and cherishing, and she would channel her love in their direction. She would be a giver of love rather than a receiver, sharing what she had rather than trying to corner the market on a piece of heaven for herself.

She reached for her pen and pad to write to Andrew. She knew he would go to her parents for consolation and she hoped her mother's oft-quoted dictum 'The pain we feel when we have more to give than others can accept is God's pain with us' would help him more than it had helped her four years ago. If she'd had this better than average figure and sexy shape, and her hair had been richly golden brown, and her face had been nice and ordinary with a couple of bonus points like her dimple and greeny-gold eyes four years ago, then she would have respected God's perfect timing. But meanwhile, the bitterness was still there . . .

She sealed up the letter, addressed it, crawled back into bed, and fell fast asleep.

CHAPTER TWO

THE early morning bell roused her from an almost drugged sleep, and she rushed to dress, and skewer back her hair with impatient hands. Why did it take longer to make herself unattractive than to present a pleasant image? She hurriedly buttoned her voluminous smock over her padded jacket and went to inspect the breakfast tables before checking off that the little future Mozarts were all diligently practising their set pieces.

As she seated herself at the Matron's table and unfurled her napkin, waiting for Grace to be sung, her eyes lit with amusement behind the thick lenses as she became aware of Valinda's penetrating stare. It was not malignant as she expected, but more wary and calculating, and somehow determined.

Breakfast over, Bridget had a word with the maids, then out of the corner of her eye she saw Valinda and Jody moving towards her with considerable effort against the flow of the rest of the girls leaving the dining-room. Bridget smiled at the maids, then speedily disappeared into her office. The girls were not going to let the grass grow under their feet, but Bridget had no desire to make things easier for them.

She let them knock twice before giving them permission to enter, hoped she was facing them with an enigmatic stare, and waited.

Valinda walked in full of confidence, but Jody was a little hesitant.

Valinda of course was the speaker. 'Miss Marlow, we've come to apologise for the whole of Washington dormitory.'

'That's exceptionally courteous of you, Valinda, and I'm very happy to accept your apologies. I hope you'll convey that news to the other girls. Now, you should hurry or you'll be late for your first period.'

Bridget bent over her charts, fully aware that there was more to come. She knew very well that if attendance at the dance was not in question she would have whistled for her apology. She was still swinging between the idea of letting the punishment stand, and earning for herself a week of unmitigated terror from Valinda and her cohorts, or revoking it because it was a little drastic. The apology had gone quite a way to mollifying her.

Valinda coughed to gain her attention. 'Miss Marlow, as I feel very responsible for the noise last night, I would like to accept all the blame and would be grateful if you would allow the rest of the dormitory to go to the dance.'

Bridget had trouble keeping the amusement from her face, but she could not but admire Valinda's strategy. To keep the six girls back when one alone admitted to being culprit was distinctly unfair, but to punish one, when all were talking, wasn't any better. She made a hasty decision more from the peace-at-any-price motive than any disciplinary ideal.

'That's very noble of you, Valinda, but I don't require a human sacrifice in order to change my mind. You may all attend the dance, but I expect exemplary behaviour for the rest of the week. You're both dismissed.'

The surprise on Valinda's face was adequate

reward. She had not expected capitulation and was no doubt primed to carry on a long and formidable engagement. One had to get up early to surprise Valinda, and Bridget felt her day had taken on a much brighter hue.

All week long the girls from Washington dorm were incredibly well behaved, and Bridget's last week on duty passed like a dream. Valinda had marshalled her forces like a general training them for battle and they volunteered for every unpleasant duty automatically. And it was not only around the boarding establishment, but in their classes and at prep that the same phenomenon was observed with grateful thanks from the teaching staff. The thought that plagued Bridget was the question of how Valinda got everyone to co-operate, not just her own dorm, because it was obvious that no one was stepping out of line, right from the juniors through to the top hierarchy. The school ran on oiled wheels. Could seven girls be responsible for all the previous chaos during the term? Reluctantly Bridget was forced to accept that theory, and was everlastingly grateful that she had tempered justice with mercy, otherwise her last week would have been one to remember with tears.

The dance was a terrific success, and against her better judgment Bridget was prevailed upon by the other staff members to attend. She had abandoned with glee her role of the drab, short-sighted, inarticulate Matron, and appeared in a shimmering gown of green and gold satin, with her hair plaited into a golden halo. She was sought after by the masters and senior boys alike and was danced off her feet, and loved every minute of it, not the least being the surprise in most people's eyes ... but not in

Jody's. Jody had always known.

Next morning amid the hustle and bustle of giving out train tickets, matching them with their owners into taxis, smiling and chatting with parents who came by car to rescue their young, she hardly sighted Jody and Valinda. Lunch was a very relaxed and pleasant affair with no more than a dozen girls left, and three mistresses. Jody and Valinda sat at the Matron's table by choice, and vied with each other to gain her attention. It was so strange. The dance was over, the term was over ... why should they bother?

Immediately after lunch they waylaid her.

'We've got a surprise for you, Miss Marlow,' Valinda offered. 'Come and see.'

Full of curiosity, Bridget followed them out of the dining-room, past the locker-rooms and out on to the street. There she stood amazed, staring at her little beat-up Morris, which was polished and shining like an old vintage car. The sun gleamed on the highly polished paintwork, and the chrome flashed blindingly in her eyes. She turned to the two in amazement. It must have taken them hours to bring about this shining perfection.

'Thank you hardly seems adequate for this effort,' she said to the grinning pair, and her own smile widened in response, showing the dimple etched so unexpectedly in her usually serious face. 'Thank you, thank you very much. But why? You didn't need to do this.'

'Yes, we did,' said Jody. 'You were awfully decent about the dance. None of the other staff would have gone back once they'd set the punishment—too scared of their image being shattered. We're grateful.'

'We wouldn't have even appealed to any of the others ... it wouldn't have been worth the effort. Anyway, I hope we get to know you better next term. That dance was a ripper!'

Bridget laughed, 'It was, wasn't it? But I won't be here next term. Didn't you know? I was only a temporary replacement.'

'Hell and damnation!' The words burst from Valinda in anger.

Bridget frowned. 'I'll excuse those words, Valinda, but only because they appear to be an expression of disappointment at my leaving.'

Valinda was still staring at her with a horrified expression. 'It's all that and more. I had a particular personal problem, and I was hoping you'd help me solve it. In fact you would have been ideal ... and now you're leaving!'

'How inconsiderate of me,' Bridget smiled at Valinda's accusing tone. 'If there's anything you want to discuss, I'm happy to help you now, Valinda.'

'You can't do anything now,' Valinda muttered disconsolately. 'I wanted to ask you if you would like to spend the summer holidays with me on a back-country station. It's a fabulous place. If I don't get a chaperon, I can't go, and I'll have to drag off to Australia with my mother. Australia I can stand, but Mother for two months I can't!'

Bridget raised an enquiring eyebrow. 'So that's how my car came to be in show-room condition ... Poor Valinda, all that wasted effort! And I probably wouldn't have considered your offer anyhow.'

Valinda had the grace to blush, then with her usual aplomb said, 'Oh, yes, you would have. I would have had all next term to show you how nice

I could be. And when I told you about this fantastic place away up in the hills, you just wouldn't have been able to refuse. Jody said you've got a special affection for the high country.'

Bridget flung a scathing glance at Jody. 'Jody has great imagination, but not a great deal of perception.'

Jody blushed crimson.

'Oh, you'd get paid, Miss Marlow. I wasn't meaning you had to do it for nothing. My father is willing to pay a handsome wage to get shot of me for two months.' Then Valinda hesitated. 'I don't suppose you'd consider it even now?'

'Perhaps I might,' Bridget surprised herself by saying. After all, she intended to stay a few months more to let Andrew get adjusted to her decision. And there was no point in rushing home to an English winter. And to be again in the mountains, with the wind song in the tussocks . . .

'*You would!*' Valinda hugged Jody in her excitement. 'Oh, fabulous! That's mighty! Oh, I can't thank you enough . . .'

'I said I'd consider it,' Bridget said crisply. 'And that's all I'm prepared to say at this moment. I may not even be in the country at Christmas time, but I'll leave my forwarding address with the Principal and you may write more fully about the place and exactly what my responsibilities would be. I have to warn you that I'm not at all enamoured with the idea of trying to be a watchdog to you, Valinda. You're an exceptionally beautiful young girl, you have an excellent brain, and many talents, but you're a natural rebel. To rebel against injustices in life is commendable, and there's plenty of scope there, but to take head-on every piece of restraint and authority in your life is a waste of energy and shows a lack of intelligence. Are you unintelligent, Valinda?'

'I'm not,' Valinda replied fiercely.

Bridget grinned. 'No, I thought not. Well, simmer down. Choose your target, attack it in an adult manner, and you could make life more pleasant for everyone. Stop creating chaos for the sheer fun of it. Taking the mickey out of the staff is . . .'

'Irresistible,' Valinda broke in impudently. 'They're so thick!'

Jody nudged her violently. 'You'd better listen to Miss Marlow if you want her to go with you.'

Valinda giggled, 'Ah, but Miss Marlow isn't thick . . .'

'And she's not soft either,' Bridget said tersely. 'If you aren't prepared to respect my authority, then don't bother getting in touch with me. Now, on your way, I have a lot of work to do. Have a good holiday, both of you, come back refreshed and restored and concentrate on your exams, instead of the all too vulnerable staff. Goodbye.'

As she walked swiftly away to the chorus of their farewells, their laughter echoed down the street, and Valinda's comment, 'You're a marvel, Jody! She's made to order—a real sweetie.'

Bridget did not feel like a sweetie. She felt she had been very foolish to even offer to consider the proposal. Valinda was trouble in anybody's language. She could not get on with her teachers or her parents. What had made her, Bridget, think she would fare any better in close combat with Valinda over a two-month period? Her words of wisdom had flowed off the girl like water off a duck's back. Still, the decision would not come for another three months, and there was something very attractive and appealing about the rebel. And there was the lure of the high country that was even more appealing.

A verse that Gareth had quoted came into her mind:

> And, high, high, the sharpened hills,
> Proud amethysts that no man tills,
> Carve pieces from the sky.

For the moment she stopped, her gaze going to the incredible beauty of the snow-covered giant Alps, glorious in the sunlight, and the brilliant blue of the sky beyond, and her heart longed with an unbearable longing to be once more in that wild and lonely part of the country, where the wind had a song all of its own, and people seemed more real and more kind than in the city.

She sighed and turned away to take up her work, knowing that barring accidents, she was going to accept Valinda's offer and return briefly to her amethyst hills, before taking up her life again. Somehow the decision brought a peace to her heart that had been long absent.

Bridget stayed on as caretaker Matron until the end of the three-week break, then moved to a small, dingy, but cheap flat in the centre of Christchurch, and counted herself fortunate to get a very boring job fitting electric components for a big firm. All day, seated at her bench, she gave all her attention to fitting the tiny pieces into place, but once home she let her mind flow towards the summertime and freedom.

She should have sought out some of her parents' friends, but did not feel any urge to do so. She spent her free time reading books on the high country, of the explorers in the early time, crossing treacherous unknown rivers and riding through wild unmapped places, and a feeling of intense excitement began building up within her. She tried to control it, repress it, reminding herself that Valinda was a highly unpredictable teenager and could have well changed her mind by now and decided to go to Australia instead, but the anticipation did not die, it only became more sweet and the desire more burning to pay this visit before going back to England. It became the centre of her whole purpose of living, and searching back in her mind she realised that for the first time in four years she was looking forward instead of looking back.

Andrew had not taken his dismissal graciously, and continued to write weekly, being utterly confident that her final decision would be in his favour. She was more grateful than ever that she had not returned immediately only to find herself under siege of his considerable persuasion and charm. His appeal was much easier to resist over a distance of several thousand miles and she answered his mail very infrequently.

Coming home one night in October she discovered a telegram in her box: 'Please contact Principal of St Matthew's urgently.' Wonderingly she walked down the road to the telephone box and put through a call to the Principal.

'Bridget Marlow here, Miss Adamson. You wanted to contact me?'

'I am grateful, Bridget, that you've been so quick to respond. Could you possibly come and see me? Tonight, if possible?'

There was an anxious urgency in her voice which

puzzled Bridget. Miss Adamson was usually so cool and formal. Had the new Matron left them in the lurch? 'Certainly, Miss Adamson. May I ask in what connection you need me?'

There was a significant pause. 'It's a very private matter and I prefer not to discuss it on the telephone. All I'm prepared to say is that it's in connection with Valinda Mason. At what time could you come?'

'I'd come tonight, Miss Adamson, but my car's in the garage.'

'Excellent. I'll send the school car for you in half an hour.'

Bridget rushed back to her flat to tidy up and tried to stem the wave of joy that was sweeping her on a full tide of excitement. How stupid she was— the school holidays were not until December, and Valinda had very important exams in November. She would not be going to the mountains yet . . . There was the car at the door.

'Do come in, Bridget. I'm so thankful you were available at a moment's notice. Valinda's father seems to have some hope that you'll have an answer for this frightful situation. He gathered from Valinda's conversation in the holidays that she holds you in high regard, and he feels if anyone can reach her now, it's you. I have to tell you I don't have the same faith. I believe Valinda has passed beyond the bounds of ordinary and decent authority and the only place for her is a detention home where she'll learn to discipline herself under a much harsher régime.'

'Valinda?' Bridget could not conceal her dismay. 'What's happened?'

'You may well ask. She's brought tragedy and

disgrace to this establishment, such as it has never suffered in its long history, and that I involve myself in her life still is more than should be expected of me.'

'I *am* asking!' Bridget almost shouted, appalled by Miss Adamson's white face and vehement tone. 'Please tell me.'

The Principal turned abruptly and walked to her desk, obviously trying to control herself. She sat down and motioned Bridget to a chair facing her. 'I truly don't know where to start. That girl has been a troublemaker ever since she arrived and I would have been well advised to listen to my senior staff last year and expel her. But she is, as you know, the daughter of a very prominent Canterbury family, and it was rather a feather in our cap that he chose St Matthew's for his daughter's education. How I wish he'd given his patronage to another school! Now, a child has died because of my indecision, and I can't forgive myself.'

'Who died?' Bridget demanded. It was obviously not Valinda.

'Jody Whitfield—a girl who showed such great promise.'

Bridget felt the tears spurt from her eyes. 'Oh, dear God, not Jody!' It seemed obscene.

'Yes, dear, little Jody. And as a direct result of wilful disobedience on Valinda's part. Valinda killed Jody. Can you imagine what it was like for me to break the news to the Whitfields?'

'I don't believe it,' Bridget muttered, as she searched for a handkerchief, unable to cope with the tears that poured down her cheeks. 'It must have been an accident. Valinda loved Jody.'

'Yes, it was an accident—a car accident. Valinda

stole a car and took Jody for a joyride and the car went out of control and crashed into a power pole, and Jody was trapped in it, while Valinda walked out without a scratch. The devil looks after his own.'

'Poor Valinda—oh, poor Valinda!' was all Bridget could say.

'Poor Valinda indeed!' There was a world of scorn in the headmistress's voice. 'If she'd shown remorse ... It took nearly an hour to free Jody from the wreck, and Valinda never cried, not once, not even at the funeral. Brazen and utterly callous.'

'Where is she now, Miss Adamson?' Bridget asked in carefully controlled tones. 'I'd like to see her.'

'She's in a cell at the Central Police Station. And I doubt if it will do you any good to see her.'

'At the police station?' Bridget felt like a parrot repeating the phrase. 'They don't lock people up for having a car accident. Why is she there?'

'Oh, she's not there because she killed Jody.' The venom in the Principal's voice suggested that she got some strange satisfaction from repeating the words, and from Bridget's stricken face. 'That happened during the first two weeks of the term. She's completely disorganised the whole school programme since then.'

Bridget fought down the desire to snap, 'Damn your school programme!' and managed to say, 'I wish you'd let me know. I would have liked to attend Jody's funeral.'

'It was in all the papers,' Miss Adamson dismissed her comment.

Bridget stopped crying and replaced her handkerchief. Something more was coming about Valinda, and she had better compose herself. She would cry for Jody later. Miss Adamson was a very good principal, kind and understanding. Something had violently shaken her, and her natural poise and mature judgment seemed to have disappeared. Only by being quiet and listening would Bridget find the information she needed to be able to help Valinda.

'Valinda's parents are overseas attending a very important conference ... a vital conference concerning the City Council, and indeed the whole economic structure of the South Island. They didn't want to return home unless it was absolutely necessary. I told them that Valinda seemed to be handling the situation calmly, but that the Board refused to allow her to remain here. Her father asked me to enter her in any other boarding school which would accept her. Well, I did try, but her record was such that no respectable school would accept her. I managed to get private board with one of her parents' friends so that she could attend a day school, and her father was very grateful. I told you he was a very influential man.'

Bridget thought savagely of what she would like to say to the very influential man who thought his conference of greater importance than rushing home to comfort his daughter.

'Yes, I do know he's made several handsome bequests to the school.'

Miss Adamson shot her a suspicious glance, but was fooled by the guileless look in Bridget's cool hazel eyes. 'Well, I thought that was the end of the matter. I felt I'd more than generously despatched my duty, and started to turn my attention to administering this school and bringing back some semblance of harmony. You realise all this was very upsetting for them all. Jody was very popular.'

'So was Valinda,' Bridget could not resist the comment.

'Valinda has no friends here. Her callous behaviour following Jody's death alienated them for ever.'

Bridget closed her eyes for a moment before answering, 'She could have been in shock.'

'I'm sorry, there was no excuse for her outrageous actions, and it sickened even her closest friends. However, I must finish this sorry story as her father has asked me to tell you, and put a proposition to you when I've done so. He's at his wits' end, poor man. He has requested that you put in a call to him in New York as soon as you've had time to make a decision.'

Bridget sat up very straight in her chair. 'Please continue, Miss Adamson.'

'I'll make it brief. Valinda gave the Blairs, where she was boarding, a hard time, a very hard time indeed. She played truant from school and was out all hours of the night, without giving any explanation. She was consorting with a very bad type, and as guardians they rang me constantly. She was running completely out of control, and I'm afraid I had no constructive advice to give them. I did go round there twice to talk with Valinda. The first time she was out, the second time she was home, but it was wasted effort. She was so hard that I couldn't get through to her. She just laughed at me . . . absolutely no respect at all. Well, I told the Blairs she was not my problem, gave them her father's overseas address, and wiped my hands of the matter. After all, I do have a school to run and there are five hundred girls in my care. I couldn't devote all my time to one incorrigible child.'

She stopped speaking and Bridget became aware

of the strain and tiredness in her eyes, and for the first time felt a little sympathy towards her. It could not have been easy. Gently she prompted, 'Then what happened?'

Wearily Miss Adamson brushed back her hair. 'The police rang me yesterday. Valinda had been arrested for selling a stolen motorbike. They'd picked her up from a pad, in a dirty condition, and the Blairs put them on to me, refusing to even discuss her time with them. They just said she'd left home and they'd listed her as missing with the police, and had no word until her arrest. They refused to visit her and said they wouldn't have her back. I went down to the station and Valinda refused to speak to me, so I rang her father. He said to contact you. He said if you were willing to take responsibility for her, you were to ring him. My advice to you is to stand well clear, and let justice take its course.'

'I couldn't do that, Miss Adamson,' Bridget said slowly. She fought back the tears that threatened again. This was no time for tears. 'I don't know what I can do. I've had no experience with difficult teenagers, and you've had years, and failed to make a breakthrough. I'll probably fail too, but I'd like to try. My parents were involved with foster-homes before they went to the Mission field. My father always said that children respond to love . . . that they may fight against it, but in the end love wins against hate. I don't come in the same category as he does when it comes to helping hurt and bewildered people, but maybe just from living with him, some of his faith and wisdom has rubbed off on me.'

Miss Adamson gave her a pitying look, 'The only one who'll end up hurt and bewildered if you go near Valinda is yourself, Bridget. I'm warning you in all seriousness.'

Bridget stood up, again fighting against the tears that threatened to overwhelm her—tears for Jody, for Valinda, for Miss Adamson, and for herself. The burden of despair and pity seemed to be like a leaden weight on her chest. 'Could I have her father's phone number, please? I would prefer to see Valinda before I ring him . . . to see if there's anything concrete I can offer. Will she go to gaol? I know nothing of the courts system here in New Zealand, or England for that matter.'

'Not gaol . . . she's too young for that. More than probably, a home for disturbed children or wayward girls. Actually the courts are very lenient and if somewhere suitable were found I'm sure the magistrate would give her a chance. It's a first offence.' Miss Adamson scribbled a phone number on a card, then a second one. 'Mr Mason said to book the call to his home number. I wish you well, Bridget. But I also wish you'd think it through . . . failure leaves an ugly taste in the mouth.'

Bridget straightened, her greeny-gold eyes bright with unshed tears. 'Failure for me, Miss Adamson, would be not to offer to help Valinda. Tell me, was there anything leading up to this trouble? Something that set her off?'

Indignantly the Principal stood up. 'I absolutely refuse to have any degree of blame attached to this school. Valinda was treated exactly the same as the others. She brought it all on herself. She's a wild, rebellious girl and I'm deeply sorry for her people.'

Bridget had reached the door, but turned. 'I'm sorry, Miss Adamson, you misunderstood me. I wasn't trying to attach blame, just trying to understand what happened to Valinda.'

The Principal was immediately mollified. 'Of course you were. Don't you think we've been over that ground a hundred times ourselves?' She walked towards Bridget and said sympathetically, 'You've sustained a severe shock, and you do look rather stricken. It's not a pretty story, and I'm sure you haven't even had your evening meal. Would you care to join us in the dining-room? You're very welcome.'

Bridget shook her head. She had no desire to share a table with those cheerful, uncomplicated brats when Valinda was in a cell. The contrast with their well fed, well dressed appearance and the comfort of their surroundings would be too vivid.

'I'm not hungry. I'll go straight round to the station. Will I have any trouble getting permission to see her?'

'No—they're expecting you. Do keep in touch, Bridget. I'll help you all I can. I want you to use the school car. It's waiting for you at the front door. Ben will wait while you're in the station and return you to your home. Tell him I insist.'

'You are kind. Goodnight.' Bridget found her throat constricted with a knot of pain. Miss Adamson *was* kind, and intelligent. If she had failed, what hope had Bridget?

She passed the message on to Ben and sank into the comfort of the luxurious upholstery. Poor Valinda, what she must have suffered to change so dramatically.

CHAPTER THREE

BRIDGET sat waiting in the interview room, feeling
almost exhausted by the effort it had required to go
through the formalities to even see Valinda. Not that
the police had been unhelpful, quite the reverse, but
as she had moved from one officer to another, each
one had added a comment to show just how un-
compromising and unco-operative Valinda had
been. She should not even be in a cell in the Central
Station but had absconded twice already from the
Home they normally kept young girls at, while
awaiting trial. She had refused to accept bail.

As Bridget heard steps approaching the door, she
straightened up. She could not let Valinda see that
she already felt defeated.

'What are you doing here?' Valinda stood in an
aggressive attitude just inside the door. 'Nobody
asked you to come.'

Bridget ignored the dirty, dishevelled clothing and
the angry, defiant eyes, and spoke quietly. 'I've just
heard of Jody's death. I thought you might like to
talk with someone else who'll miss her.'

'I don't miss her.'

'I'm sure you do. You two were inseparable . . .'

'Were we?' Valinda jeered bitterly. 'The system
separated us with no trouble at all.'

'I don't understand,' said Bridget. 'Could you tell
me?'

'Why should I? What do you care? You're just
here to try and make me bawl all over the place and

say I'm sorry she was topped. Well, I won't, so you may as well leave.'

Bridget felt a shiver go down her spine at the ugly way Valinda had described Jody's death. She was hard, but behind the savageness in her eyes was pain and fear. 'Why haven't you cried for Jody, Valinda?' she asked.

'Why should I cry? I don't miss her.' Valinda's laughter was shrill. 'That's what you lot don't understand. To me Jody is alive. She always will be. As long as I keep her in my mind, she can't die. And she'll live for ever, believe me!'

Bridget closed her eyes for a moment so that Valinda could not see the pity there. Poor scared girl! She believed that if she cried and grieved for Jody, then Jody would die. She just was not prepared to accept Jody's death, that way she did not have to accept any responsibility for it. No wonder her behaviour had been considered bizarre! How could she get through to her? 'Yes, I believe you, Valinda. I believe Jody will live for ever too, but not in the same way you do. Does my coming here bother you, Valinda? You've got a lot of trouble on your plate, and I don't want to add to it. You've already been hurt enough.'

'You can stay if you want to. You can go if you want to. You're not hurting me . . . nobody can, not ever again. I mean that.'

'I'm glad of that,' said Bridget quietly. 'Well, I would like to stay a bit longer, if it's not bothering you, but I can't if you're going to stand all the time. Come and sit on the couch beside me and relax . . . or can't you relax?' She held her breath, knowing she had made her offer a deliberate challenge.

Valinda's eyes glittered. 'Why shouldn't I be able

to relax? Do you think I'm scared of you?' She stormed across the room and flung herself on the couch.

Bridget breathed again. She had been so scared that Valinda would rush from the room. 'Tell me, Valinda, what you meant by that earlier remark about the system separating you from Jody. Miss Adamson never mentioned anything . . .'

'Of course she didn't, the old bat! If it hadn't been for her, and her stupid regulations, Jody would be . . . we would never have been riding in the damn car.'

So there had been something to start Valinda off. 'Tell me, please,' invited Bridget.

Valinda stared at her suspiciously for a moment, as if undecided whether to continue talking or not, then it poured from her. 'Well, Jody stayed with me during the holidays. You knew she was going to stay with me. And we talked a lot about you. And we talked a lot about what you said about baiting teachers just for the fun of it, and it did seem a bit pathetic. We both wanted our University Entrance so we could get to hell out of the place, so we decided we'd work our guts out and try and make up the time we'd wasted fooling around. We knew we had no hope of being accredited—well, I didn't, and Jody didn't want to go without me . . .'

Her voice trailed off as she realised that Jody had done just that, and there was a deep silence. Valinda stared at the carpet and the silence stretched to an almost agonised length.

Suddenly she flung back her head and her eyes were dark with pain, but her voice was harsh. 'So we meant to make a bird of it. And we made a list of all the really dumb rules. We weren't stupid, we knew you've got to have some organisation for a mob that size, but there are some things at that school that are ridiculous, and if we had any spare time we were going to try to change them ... in an adult way, like you said. Not by getting in Old Adam's hair, but by getting the girls together and discussing it and voting on it, then writing out a petition. We had a lot of fun planning it. Then Jody went home for the last week ...'

Again her voice trailed off and Bridget saw her eyes were blank as if she was back in the holidays. Bridget felt guilty as she remembered thinking her words had just washed over Valinda. She had been wrong. Those two kids had really spent a lot of time sorting themselves out. So what had happened?

'Then school started and it was fun in a way to be back, great to be with Jody, and we giggled about the shock they were going to get when they had to adjust to our new image. And it never happened, you see.' A new bitterness crept into Valinda's voice. 'We hadn't reckoned on Old Adam doing a bit of thinking herself over the holidays. People like her shouldn't think. It can be too dangerous, they haven't got the required equipment. You're a missionary's daughter, aren't you? Do you know what the Old Adam means?'

Bridget was puzzled. 'Well, it's supposed to be that part of us that still belongs to the devil.'

'Right! And she does.' Valinda was vicious. 'She was well named. She gave us just a day together, and we hadn't put a foot wrong, then she comes up with her great idea. If Jody and I were to have any hope of getting U.E. we had to be separated—for our own good, *of course*. Jody got sent up to the new senior block, you know, across the road. They have

their own lounge, and prep rooms, and are allowed
to make their own supper, real mind-boggling stuff.
She had to share a room with that creep Denter.
She hated it and I hated it. We never got to see
each other after school. We were put in different
teams, not even allowed to have our meals together,
or music practice; hers was in the Gym from seven
till eight in the morning and mine in the Library
eight till nine, and we were put in different streams,
Jody stayed with A and I moved back to B, so we
didn't even see each other in class . . .'

Bridget was appalled. 'So when did you see each
other?'

'Never. It was very effective.' Outrage and pain
were naked in Valinda's voice. 'Saturdays and
Sundays were done the same. There was no way,
you see . . . nothing we could do. We did go to Old
Adam and tell her what we'd worked out, I mean
about trying for U.E., and asked her could she give
it a trial, but she just laughed. Said we'd left our run
too late . . .'

Bridget sighed, 'Oh, Valinda, I'm so sorry! I know
how close you were. It must have been awful.'

'That's not the word for it. It was hell. Then that
Saturday we got a couple of minutes after lunch together at the front gate, and there was a car sitting
there with the key in it, and I asked Jody if she'd
like to go for a spin and have a couple of hours
together, and she was always game for anything . . .
Well, we breezed off . . . it was a fantastic car,
handled like a dream. We didn't do anything wrong
. . . just went up on the hill and sat in the sun and
talked and talked.' Valinda stopped speaking.

Bridget was silent too, thinking of those two friends
so desperate for some time together, enjoying the sun,

the sea, and just time to talk. Of course the Principal had reasons for the action she had taken, but she had no need to be so drastic. Even the dormitory shift would have been traumatic on its own, but the rest sounded almost like victimisation, with no right of redress. Poor psychology, but what a price to pay!

'Well, she can't take that away,' Valinda went on. 'It was mighty. Then it started to get dark and we thought we'd better go home and face the enemy, but then I struck a patch of oil on the road, and the car went out of control and hit a power pole, and crashed down the side of a hill. I got thrown out, and Jody was . . .'

'Killed,' Bridget said softly. 'You'd better accept it, Valinda, or you can't go on.'

'I won't! I won't! There's nothing to go on for, without Jody.'

'I didn't think you were a coward, Valinda. I thought you had guts.'

'I *have* too. You know, she believed in God. What sort of a God would crush the life out of a sweet kid like Jody? He's supposed to take care of kids.'

'That's exactly what he does,' said Bridget. 'And I'm glad Jody was a Christian. I know exactly where she is now and I'm happy for her.'

'Oh, *you*!' Valinda spat the words out. 'You're like all those other sanctimonious creeps at the funeral . . . God's will . . . she's gone to a better place . . . rubbish! What about *me*? Why didn't he take me too?' The cry was from the heart, and then came the tears, cascading down Valinda's dirty face, and her body was shaking with grief.

Bridget gathered her into her arms, not trying to stop her own crying or Valinda's. They were Jody's friends; it was right that they should grieve together.

And she was just so thankful that Valinda had broken down. When this was over she would see what they could build up together.

At last the racking sobs ceased, and Valinda's crying was more controlled, quieter, but Bridget still continued to rock her gently in her arms until the whole dammed-up force of pain, hurt, and guilt was drained away in the healing tears of natural grief. It took a long time, but Bridget did not want to hurry the process. She could hardly bear to think of the burden Valinda had carried ever since the accident, and she would *not* think of the Principal. Everyone made mistakes, and in theory it probably looked sensible to part the children, but it was hard to forgive the sheer bloody-mindedness that had carried the idea to such lengths.

Valinda sat up, scrubbing at her eyes, and Bridget put a clean handkerchief into her hand. 'Sorry about that, Miss Marlow.'

'Bridget is the name, if you want to use it.'

There was a flicker of the old impudence for a second, 'I know. We used to call you Frigid Bridget.' Valinda shrugged her slight shoulders. 'I'm sorry about that. Seems I've got a lot to be sorry about.'

'Don't be. It was appropriate. Would you like a cup of coffee? I'll ask the constable on duty. I'm sure he'd bring one.'

Valinda nodded, so Bridget made the request, then turned back to find Valinda stretched out on the couch with her hand across her eyes. Her face was pale and yet she seemed relaxed.

'You okay?' Bridget enquired.

'Yes. Just tired . . . so tired. Do you really believe all that guff you fed me, about knowing where Jody is . . . that she's all right?' There was a wistfulness in the tone as if she longed to believe Bridget.

'Positive,' Bridget said firmly.

'Seems funny, Jody being happy without me. You sort of grow close when you're locked up in the same loony-bin for four years. Why didn't He take me too if He's such a good guy?' Valinda's voice was gruff.

'I can't answer that, Valinda. Just that it was Jody's time, and it wasn't yours. There must be something else you have to do with your life.'

'What's the purpose and plan for your life?' Valinda moved her hand so that she could watch Bridget's face.

'I don't know yet,' Bridget answered honestly. 'I thought I did once, but I came unstuck. I lost someone I loved as much as you loved Jody. I went a bit crazy for a while, but I came right. You will too, but it takes time.'

'How old were you?' Valinda demanded.

'Seventeen.'

'I was seventeen last week.' Valinda was still watching her carefully. 'How long did you take to come right?'

Bridget hesitated, then decided again on honesty. 'Well, the crazy bit lasted about six months, but the cure about four years, I guess, and I'm still working on it.'

Valinda nodded, 'Yeah, I guess it will take a long time.'

A glimmer of a smile lit Bridget's eyes. 'It won't take you as long as it did me. You're much more mature than I was at your age, and of course, more intelligent.'

Valinda grinned back, 'Of course.'

There was a knock on the door and a young uniformed man came in carrying a tray with coffee and sandwiches. He gave Valinda a sharp look, then seemed satisfied, and placed the tray on the table. 'Sing out if you want more coffee.'

'Thanks,' Bridget smiled at him. 'Is it all right if I stay a bit longer?'

'Yes. The sergeant said to take as long as you want.'

Bridget's hand flew to her mouth. 'Oh, I'd forgotten all about Ben! He's sitting out there in the St Matthew's School car. He must be tired. Is it too much to ask that you thank him for me and tell him to go home? It's parked directly opposite the front door.'

'Sure, I'll fix that for you.'

Bridget handed Valinda her coffee, and took a cup herself. Neither of them wanted to eat.

'What happens now?' Valinda asked vaguely, as if it really had nothing to do with her. 'I've got to appear in court tomorrow.'

'I don't know, but I'll find out. I think a lot depends on you. You could end up on probation, or perhaps be sent to reform school. I have to ring your father tonight. He's very anxious about you . . .'

'About his good name,' Valinda offered with a little of the bitterness back in her voice. She sipped her coffee. 'Can't blame him really. I've somewhat blotted the family escutcheon . . . he didn't deserve that.'

'Don't you get on with either of your parents? That's sad.'

'Not sad. You haven't met them. Dad does try, I'll give him that, and I try with him, sometimes. But we just don't make it. We never could. I'm not his kid, you see.'

'Of course you are,' Bridget protested. 'That's a silly thing to say.'

'It's true,' Valinda said quite unemotionally. 'I've known for years. Don't look so shocked. Mother got bored once my two brothers and sisters started school, and had what's termed a little fling. I was the result. I heard them fighting one night, yelling the place down one night after a party. Oh, they don't know that I know. Guess they hung together for the sake of the family name, or money, or position. All I know is, it wasn't love. I didn't tell anyone, except Jody. She understood.'

Bridget decided to leave the subject alone. 'About tomorrow—I think if someone were to offer to take responsibility for you, you could walk out of the courtroom tomorrow . . . as it's a first offence.'

'Who'd be that dumb?' Valinda scoffed.

'I would,' Bridget offered. 'That's if you were willing to live with me, until your parents come home. But you'd have to go back to school. You'd want . . .'

'No deal,' Valinda said harshly. 'I'd rather move back in with the gang than face school again. Forget it.'

Bridget did not let on how worried she was. 'Well, you and Jody planned on showing Miss Adamson that you could get your U.E. Why not give it a try? Couldn't you study at home?'

'No, I'd never make it. There's correspondence lessons, but you can only get them if you're handicapped in some way . . . or live in an isolated place.'

Bridget waited. It was better if Valinda came up with the solution. If anything was going to work, it had to have her approval. Whatever decision was made, it was not going to be easy. Valinda had been through too much too fast for life to run smoothly.

'I've got it!' Valinda's eyes were bright. 'I just said it—you have to live in an isolated place. Well, I asked you if you'd come with me at Christmas to the station, Paradise Peaks. If we could go now, they might let me do a correspondence course. It's a bit late, but I'd give it a whirl . . . I'd try my damnedest. I owe Jody that much. It would be great to see Old Adam's face if I did make it.'

'It might work,' Bridget answered cautiously. 'Who lives there? Would they be prepared to have us to stay? I mean, after this trouble . . .'

'My great-aunt owns it. And Dad is her blue-eyed boy. She's a real character . . . tough as old boots. And there's plenty of rooms. She lives in a great mansion, that's the only thing she spends money on. Dad and her are always arguing, but she won't let him bully her. She lets the station land go hang and keeps the house great. She's got a married couple, about as old as herself, to cook and keep the garden. It's a fabulous place, thirty thousand acres of mountains and tussock and rivers and hardly a fence on it—beautiful!'

She stared at Bridget and her face went still. 'Forget it. Your expression gives you away. I'll go to Borstal or whatever. I can see you don't fancy being holed up in the hills with me for a couple of months. Can't say I blame you . . .'

'Don't be childish! I'm just trying to think my way through. You seem to forget that you're up on a charge. We must have something feasible to offer. I'm quite prepared to go with you if your father can arrange it, but there's not much time. I'll go and ring him now. But don't get your hopes up too high. The magistrate has to be convinced that it's in your best interests, that you're going to be under proper control, that you're not going to run wild and get into further bother. He may not think much of my credentials. He may feel that someone older . . .'

'There isn't anyone older than my aunt. How about you getting back in that gear you wore at school? That would convince anybody that I wasn't going to have any fun with you. You used to look awful.'

'Thank you, Valinda,' said Bridget wryly, 'but I have no intention of wearing that. I'll ring your father and listen to what he has to say. I'll be guided by his experience of court procedure. I have no idea really, of what will happen. Now, I suggest you go out there and co-operate fully with the police. It could make all the difference to what the magistrate's decision will be. If they say you've been undisciplined and aggressive, he may think you need stronger corrective training. You've got a lot of leeway to make up, I believe.'

Valinda stood up. 'Thank you, Bridget. I don't know what made you come, but I'm glad you did. I'll do anything if you get me out of this.'

Bridget regarded her thoughtfully. 'I'm glad I came. I know it's been tough, and it could become a lot tougher. I have to say this, Valinda, and I hope you won't be upset. Before I take responsibility for you, or even offer to, I must know if you're going to behave reasonably. You see, I can't become your jailer; I'd like to be your friend. You haven't responded to authority very well in the past, and once I become the authority in your life, you may come to resent me too, and I would hate that.'

'It won't happen, Miss Marlow . . . sorry, Bridget. I promise you, I give my word.'

'I don't believe it will, Valinda, I think we'll get

along fine, but don't make any rash promises. Just say you'll give it your best shot, and I'll be satisfied. We've come a long way together, tonight.'

'We sure have.' Valinda's eyes filled with tears. 'I'll give it my best shot. I am grateful.'

'I'm not looking for your gratitude. I'll give it my best shot too, and I think we'll be an unbeatable combination.' Bridget leaned forward and gave Valinda a quick hug. 'See you tomorrow. God bless you!'

Sitting in court next morning, Bridget was amazed just how much Mr Mason had accomplished over the phone since she had spoken to him. His personal lawyer had just finished telling her that he had already arranged with Miss Adamson to apply to the Correspondence School for work, stressing the urgency of its arrival and that they would duplicate some work Valinda had missed so that she would have something to start on. Also on Mr Mason's instructions he had contacted the general manager of the firm where Bridget was working to smooth out any difficulties about her sudden resignation, which was a tremendous relief to her.

Arranging bail would pose no problems, as the great-aunt had been only too eager to help her nephew in his trouble, and Bridget was to speak with Mr Mason again immediately after the case was heard, and was to try and persuade Valinda to speak to him too. Money and influence certainly were helping, but she conceded that she had been impressed with Mr Mason and his penetrating yet swift assessment of her character, his unstinting approval of her approach to Valinda's problem, and his succinct summing up of the situation. Even that relatively short conversation over the long distance gave her some insight into his powerful and forthright personality, and reversed some of her rather hastily formed judgments of his actions.

One by one the cases were heard, and Bridget was glad of the company of an attractive woman wearing a badge inscribed 'Friends at Court' who explained the procedure to her. She was also glad that she had remembered to rush a change of clothes round for Valinda, when she saw her standing in the dock, her face pale and tense, yet calm as she searched the public bench for Bridget. Reassured by Bridget's smile, she turned to give her attention to the magistrate and the court proceedings.

It was over so swiftly that Bridget was astonished. The charge was read by a policeman, the lawyer spoke, and the magistrate listened attentively, consulted with the clerk about the date set for the next hearing, and the police to see if they had any objection to bail being given. He then admonished Valinda in an almost fatherly fashion, warning her that her behaviour over the next six weeks would almost certainly have a great deal of bearing on the sentence she would receive at her next appearance.

Valinda was very quiet and thoughtful as they waited in the administration offices to have the bail notices typed and signed. Her face was serious, almost stern, as they walked in the warm spring sunshine towards the Cathedral Square, and Bridget hesitated to speak in case she struck the wrong note. With unspoken consent they both leaned on the wide concrete balustrade of the bridge over the Avon river and watched the ducks swimming and diving in the pretty stream, bordered attractively with green weeping willows and sloping grass banks.

'I suppose Daddy has been busy pulling all the

right strings.' Valinda's voice was colourless.

'I don't know about pulling strings, Valinda, but he's tried to make things easy for you.'

'And him. He must have been vastly relieved to have someone like you to volunteer to take responsibility for me. A quick phone call here and there, a palm greased, and he can then turn his attention to the more important things of life.'

'Don't think like that, Valinda. He really cares for you. I spoke to him last night, and that was quite clear—not his position, but yours' dear.' Bridget longed to put an arm around the slender, fragile girl, but could not. This was not the time; there was a remoteness and sadness there which it would have been an impertinence to break.

'So he took you in too, and over the telephone . . . wait till you meet him in the flesh. As the papers say, a 'dynamic personality'. Of course he cares about me, but not in the way you imply. He has to protect me, to protect himself. Imagine what the voters would say if he didn't show himself as the poor bewildered daddy of a wayward daughter! This may even earn him votes, treated sympathetically, as they so cutely say in the Public Relations Office.'

'Would it help if he came home?' Bridget asked.

'Not in the least . . . as I said, he tries, I try, but we fail.'

'Well, seeing you admit he tries, will you do something to please him? He's really been active in setting up this station idea of yours, and he would like to talk with you. I have to ring him now. Will you come along to the Square and just thank him for the arrangements he's made?'

Valinda pushed herself away from the bridge. 'Sure, but only because you'll be upset if I don't.'

Let's get it over with, and get out of Christchurch.'

'Today?' Bridget asked in surprise.

'Why not? Have you anything special that would keep you? Valinda sounded a little impatient.

'Well, no. My car's in the garage. I can collect it after lunch. But I thought it would take a few days to get our things together. I suppose we could . . .'

'Of course we could. You drop me off at the Blairs', where I was boarding, and I'll pick up some gear and take a taxi round home to get the rest. You can meet me there when you've packed.' Valinda walked swiftly in the direction of the Square.

Bridget followed her, feeling once again the immensity of the task she had taken on. What on earth had made her think she would be able to influence a girl who had matched strengths with her parents, teachers, and even the police? Why, she had almost taken control already! Bridget quickened her step and reached the toll counter of the Post Office a second behind Valinda.

'You did say we were calling Daddy from here, didn't you? Have you got his number?' Valinda held out her hand.

Giving Valinda a cool look, Bridget said, 'I have the number in my bag, and I'll put the call in.'

She searched in her bag, pulled the card out and gave her request to the clerk, wondering why her legs were so shaky. Was it always going to be like this—one moment sharing the suffering with Valinda, the next wanting to slap her for behaving like a brat? She would have to become more assertive, make a stand . . .

Valinda eyed her shrewdly. 'You look a bit ghastly. Getting cold feet? Not exactly leaning forward in the saddle, are you?'

Not by a flicker of her long eyelashes did Bridget let Valinda know how close she was to hitting the mark. 'I look ghastly because I'm starving to death. I missed dinner last night, missed breakfast this morning, and no matter how urgently you want to leave town, I refuse to miss lunch. Do you want to speak first or shall I?'

'I will, and I'll be brief.'

After a few minutes Bridget accepted the phone, and was immediately warmed by the sincerity of Mr Mason's thanks.

'Right, Bridget, you're in complete control. I have warned Valinda that if she steps out of line you're to notify the police and they'll resume authority. I was telling Valinda, too, that there's been considerable change out at Paradise Peaks, Aunt Grace was finally forced to take the trustees' advice and put in a good manager. She should have done it years ago, but she's a very obstinate old lady. She's wasted the land. It's almost reverted to its original state, but this Evans chappie will change all that . . .'

Bridget only heard the name Evans and the rest of the sentence was lost to her. 'What's his first name?' She asked the question urgently, but her voice was so low that she had to repeat it.

'Sorry, I can't tell you that,' said Mr Mason. 'You'll meet him soon enough. Valinda says you're going there this afternoon. I'm pleased he's there, for your sake. He'll be a tower of strength . . . has an excellent reputation. First-class bloke. Now, feel free to ring me at any time. I'm fully conscious of the debt I owe you for stepping into the breach with so little warning. I'll keep you acquainted with my whereabouts as I move around, and you mustn't hesitate to call if any further problems arise. Is that understood?'

'Yes, thank you,' was all that Bridget could manage. What if it turned out to be Gareth Evans? *Her* Gareth Evans? No, that was quite impossible. Or was it?

'You also mentioned your father last night, wishing you had his experience. Draw on it. Book any calls to my number. Understand?'

'Yes, and thank you.'

'You sound a bit shaken,' said Mr Mason. 'Has Valinda been getting at you? Put her back on, I'll have another word with her.'

'No, it's nothing like that. Probably a bad connection.' Bridget listened to some further instructions, then with relief put the phone back on the hook and joined Valinda.

'Daddy shake you up a bit, too?'

'No, I . . .'

'Oh, I forgot you haven't eaten. I'm a bit hungry myself. Come on Bridget, we'll go and eat. You'd better make the most of it, food out there is fairly basic.'

Bridget followed Valinda out into the sunshine and across the square to a small attractive restaurant, and sat blankly while the lunch was ordered, forgetting completely her intention to assert herself. She was in a blind panic. Even if Mr Mason had said it was Gareth Evans there was no way out for her. She had undertaken in a court of law to take Valinda to the station. How could she avoid it? Her mind seemed to be made of cottonwool. Imagine trying to explain her objection to say . . . Valinda, or worse, Mr Mason. She would sound ridiculous.

She forced herself to eat in spite of the fact that

everything tasted like cardboard, and was relieved
that Valinda appeared to prefer silence too. Even
that observation made Bridget feel guilty, she should
have been extending herself to lift the sadness from
Valinda's young face, and all she could do was think
of her own predicament. How selfish she was!
Especially as it was probably all in her own wild
imagination.

Gareth was most certainly back in the North
Island in partnership with his father and brother in
that huge farming complex. As a married man he
would hardly be likely to take his wife and children
to an isolated region when he had such a golden
opportunity already reserved for him. The thought
brought her a semblance of calm.

An hour later, when she called at the Mason re-
sidence for Valinda, she was firmly in control of herself and able to appreciate the beauty and elegance
of the house and grounds. To have a background
like that and yet so little happiness seemed incredibly
sad.

'You can't take all that, Valinda!' Bridget gazed at
the three huge cases by the front door. 'I simply
haven't got the room, and you won't need many
clothes. I'm only taking one case, but seeing you
have a lot of books for study, I'll let you take two,
but that's the limit.'

Valinda shrugged her shoulders, 'I couldn't think
what to take, so I put everything in. Come and help
me sort it out.'

Bridget slid from the car, her sympathy immediately aroused by the drawn, resigned expression. Valinda seemed to have lost the energy she had
had this morning when she forced the decision to
leave. 'I shouldn't have left you on your own, pet.

Never mind, we'll soon have it repacked.'

She carried the cases back into the lounge and while Valinda sat in a chair watching, she quickly repacked the minimum requirements. 'Anything else you want? There's a little space left.'

'Better throw in another couple of dresses. Aunt Grace likes everyone to change out of jeans into something decent for dinner. Any two will do, there's no one to impress out there. Old Jim, who manages the place in a haphazard fashion, borrows a couple of musterers from the next station for a few days each spring, and they usually have a couple of callow youths to help with the tailing and odd jobs. His wife, Jess, is cook—if you can call it that. She's used to Aunt Grace's ways, but when she slings the food on the table I always feel like commenting, "Untouched by human hands".'

'So what's the attraction?' asked Bridget. 'Obviously not the company.'

'Dunno. But I like it there.'

Bridget looked up suddenly as she finished shutting the case and saw Valinda's blue eyes brimming with tears. 'It will work out, Valinda. Now let's get on the road. You take the extra case back up to your room, and I'll put these in the car. Make sure you lock the house securely.'

As they drove off, Bridget said, 'We have to call at St Matthew's to pick up your work load . . .'

'I'm not going to see Old Adam,' announced Valinda.

'You don't have to, I'll hop in and get it. But if by any chance she comes out to the car, I'll expect you to be polite. She's prepared this work which you'll need. That was generous of her. Can't you match her?'

'No. I hate her. I'd like to kill her, slowly and painfully.'

Bridget sighed as she swung the car into the school drive. 'Try and forgive her, Valinda. She made a wrong decision, but she couldn't see what the result of that decision would be. If you hold bitterness against her, it won't really hurt her, but your nature will be altered. Hatred or resentment held in the heart eats into your soul, and warps the personality. Don't let her do that to you, Valinda. She's not worth it. Try feeling sorry for her.'

'Me feel sorry for her? Why should I?' Valinda demanded aggressively.

Bridget parked by the front steps. 'You're intelligent, work it out for yourself.' She ran quickly up the steps, hoping against hope that Miss Adamson would be content to give her the papers and let her go. But she was not so lucky. Miss Adamson wanted to know everything about the trial, wanted to warn Bridget again about making such a rash move, and wanted to restate her opinion of certain failure.

Bridget listened because she had to wait for the papers, then explaining that they were in a hurry to get up country before dark, she tried to make a hasty exit. Again she was foiled and Miss Adamson followed her out to the car, where she proceeded to lecture Valinda, who apart from a brief greeting, accepted the flow of words impassively.

Bridget switched on the engine and leaned across Valinda to say a final thank you, then let out the clutch with real thankfulness.

Valinda waited until Bridget turned right and headed towards the South Road. 'You're right, she's more to be pitied than hated. You're a pretty sneaky player, aren't you, Bridget Marlow?'

'I'm not,' Bridget protested.

'Yes, you are. You knew that if I was rude I'd never hear what she was trying to say. I can accept the blame for my part in what happened, but she can't accept any blame. She wants me to carry it all. She's got no intestinal fortitude, as my father would say. She's just a front, all bluster and blather, no depth. No, I wouldn't kill her. As you say, she's not worth it. Why are you driving south?' added Valinda.

'To get out of town,' Bridget answered, somewhat surprised.

'Well, you will too, but you're heading in the wrong direction. Don't you know where Paradise Peaks Station is?'

Bridget swung into the side of the road with a laugh. 'Now that you come to mention it, nobody has told me where it is. I just presumed it was south out of the city.'

Valinda grinned, 'I could really lead you up the garden path, couldn't I? But I won't. Here, give me that map. Paradise Peaks is right in the mountains, at the foot of the Lewis pass, see. We head out on the main north road.'

'Why, that's hundreds of miles away from ...' Bridget stopped short, remembering that Valinda knew nothing of her stay in the high country down near Lake Wanaka.

'Hundreds of miles from where?' Valinda asked.

'Hundreds of miles from where I thought it was,' Bridget laughed again. Oh, the sweet relief of finding she was going to live miles and miles and lovely miles from where she had spent the summer months with Gareth years ago.

Valinda was giggling now, but managed to gasp,

'And *you're* supposed to be looking after me! And *you* don't even know where you're driving!'

They both laughed until the tears ran down their faces. It seemed so silly. As the healing laughter subsided, Bridget studied the map and charted a new course.

'I'll drive if you like,' Valinda offered. 'I'll get us there in half the time because I know the way.'

'You'll do no such thing. You know your licence has been revoked until your trial.'

'You're not going to be all that stuffy, surely? Nobody will know.'

'I will,' said Bridget firmly. 'And if not letting you drive makes me stuffy, then that's exactly what I am.'

'I thought you might be.' There was no hint of resentment in Valinda's voice.

'Will you do something for me, Valinda? I mean without asking a whole reef of questions. It's important to me or I would not ask.'

'Shoot.'

'I beg your pardon? Oh, I see. I would prefer that no one knows I'm the daughter of a missionary, so I'm asking you not to mention the fact.'

'Why?' Valinda gave her a sharp look. 'You're not ashamed of it, are you?'

'You know better than that. It's for a very stupid private reason which I'd prefer not to explain just now. I may tell you later.'

'No sweat. I'll be the proverbial clam.'

'Good.' Bridget concentrated on her driving with renewed pleasure. She had covered all bets. She felt now that Gareth Evans was not the new manager, but just in case he was, it would be too easy a lead for him to piece together, if she was introduced as

Miss Marlow, a missionary's daughter.

She put him out of her mind. She had enough problems without adding imaginary ones.

CHAPTER FOUR

ALL through the spring-green plains, and up among the golden tussock hills, the little car ran beautifully. Ahead, snow was burnished by the late sunlight to a coppery glow, and bush began to cast out fringes and then shawls over the golden hills.

'We're nearly in the mountains, how much farther?' Bridget asked.

'Through this bush, then up a short rise, and we'll come out on a tussock flat. At the end of that, about half a mile, we swing on to a private road—it's only a gravel road. It takes about half an hour from here. Look at the setting sun on the snow. Fabulous!'

'It is indeed. Oh, I've loved this drive, really loved it!'

'Turn here,' Valinda instructed. 'See, there's the mail-box.'

Bridget saw the yellow and black A.A. signpost with *Paradise Peaks No Exit*, printed on it, and back came that empty edge of fear. No Exit meant no way out, abandon hope all ye who enter here. It was just the uncertainty. She would be fine as soon as she found out just who Evans, the manager, was.

'Are you tired, Valinda?' she asked. 'This day seems to have gone on for ever.'

'Yes, I'll be glad to get there.'

The narrow gravel road wound up through the beautiful birch forest, then suddenly came out into the late afternoon sunlight and Bridget feasted her eyes on a glorious open valley, so vast and wide that there seemed no end to it.

Sheep grazed on the river flats, and high on a plateau sat the homestead, a green oasis in the tawny tussocks. A river ran like a silver and blue thread against the rocky bluffs on the far left and above that the heavy bush-clad hills, which gave way again to a magnificent range of snow-capped peaks.

'Paradise Peaks,' Valinda offered. 'It stops most people in their tracks. In one of Great-Grandfather's old diaries he described riding from Christchurch to take up this land, and when he saw it, he wanted to call it Heaven-Sent, his Promised Land. He named the river Jordan. Those three hills are called Peter, Paul and Luke. Aunt Grace said they always stopped here with the wagons when she was little and she thought it was to give the horse a spell, but when they got cars they did the same. It's automatic—the way you did.'

It was only then Bridget realised that she had stopped. 'It's tremendous.' Beyond the homestead the golden tussock foothills only led the eyes on to deep purple-shadowed granite giants. Her amethyst hills. She started the car and drove on towards the house almost hidden in the trees from this angle.

The first Curtis had provided the Station with a splendid homestead of magnificent proportions. On sweeping lawns sprinkled with daffodils, large old English trees and New Zealand native trees added to the beauty of the architecture and the grace of the flourishing flower-beds.

'How many rooms does it have, Valinda? It could house an army, and take an army to keep it clean.'

'Twelve, I think—no, there's more, counting the servants' quarters. They really lived in style, but I'm glad I wasn't the downstairs maid—talk about cramped quarters! Wait till you see the ballroom. It's been kept just as it was when Aunt Grace was young, but she's shut up the west wing. They used to entertain a lot, but over the years she's lost touch with her friends, and fought with all the relations except Daddy, so no one comes now.'

A deep veranda ran along the front of the house, with glass doors leading off it. Bridget pulled up in front, feeling her small, shabby Morris must have a distinct inferiority complex being parked so close to such splendour.

'Do we sit here and wait for a horde of servants to line the steps and welcome us?' she asked.

Valinda giggled, 'You'll wait a long time. We'll have to heft our own luggage.'

Carrying a case in each hand, Bridget climbed the steps and followed Valinda in the massive front door, then gasped, dropping the luggage. The hall was a stately fifty-by-twenty-foot room with an elegant moulded, gently arched ceiling, and a sweeping staircase leading away to the right. Great bowls of freesias stood on either side.

Valinda was not overawed in any way. 'Anybody home?' she yelled in a voice which would have been better suited to a barrack room. 'Put your cases down, Bridget, and I'll give you a swift tour. I haven't seen it since it was redecorated. Daddy said it's incredible.'

She flung the door on their left open. 'Reception room.' And without giving Bridget time to draw breath, she crossed it and slid back beautifully panelled double doors. 'Ballroom.' Bridget gained a fleeting impression of crystal chandeliers, bright flowers and highly polished wooden floors before Valinda was again on her way.

Valinda's impudent grin showed she was well aware of Bridget's astonishment. 'Impressed?' she queried.

'That's one word for it. All that space, all that luxury, for just one old lady to use.'

'Wrong, she doesn't use it—just looks at it, dresses it up and remembers happier days. Here's the library, and now I'll take you out to the kitchen and lounge which are the only rooms used apart from the bedrooms. She spends all her time gardening, anyway.'

'Hullo,' a sweet childish voice called from the stairs. 'Who are you?'

Valinda stared in surprise. 'Who are you?'

'I'm Telly. I live here with Mummy and Gareth and Matthew and . . .'

'The heck you do!' Valinda was quite upset. 'I wonder who they are? Sounds like an invasion!'

Bridget went white. Was this Gareth's child? 'Hullo, Kelly, I'm Bridget, and this is Valinda. We're going to stay here too.'

Kelly came flying down the stairs, a fairylike child about three years old. 'Good, I'm a big girl, and Matthew is only little. Mummy's in the kitchen. This is her house.'

'Is it indeed?' Valinda strode forward. 'We'll see about that!'

Bridget took Kelly's proffered hand and followed more slowly. Valinda was talking to the sweetest old lady with silver-grey hair and bright blue eyes, 'Oh, here she is, Aunt Grace. This is Bridget Marlow. Bridget, meet my Great-Aunt Grace.'

Bridget looked at the dainty elegance of Miss Curtis and felt more like dropping a curtsey than offering her hand. 'Thank you for giving us sanctuary,' she said.

Miss Curtis smiled, 'It's a great pleasure to have you with us. You are, of course, far too young to be in charge of Valinda, but that's your problem. I hope you will enjoy your stay. Now come and meet Kathy and Gareth. I've just finished explaining to Valinda that I have a new manager, Gareth Evans. Poor old Jim had a stroke three months ago, and Jess refused to stay out here in case he took another one. As if moving to Christchurch would prevent having a second one! So I was advised to take Gareth on— no, that's incorrect ... I was forced to take him. That interfering busybody of a lawyer of mine had me over a barrel. For years he's tried to get me to put on a progressive man, and this time he refused to give me money for a house for Jim and Jess unless I agreed.'

The door opened and there stood a lovely young woman of about twenty-four, with dark curly hair and a charming smile. 'I thought I heard voices, so I popped the kettle on again. Would you like afternoon tea in the lounge or the kitchen, Miss Curtis?'

'The kitchen—don't fuss. Oh, Valinda, this is Kathy. She looks after me in quite a wonderful fashion. You've met Kelly, now come and meet Matthew.'

The kitchen was enormous, with exposed beams and large windows that looked out on the mountains beyond. It had an air of old-fashioned warmth yet included the very latest labour-saving devices. A double-ovened oil cooker sent out a cheerful glow, flowers peeped out of corners and at the far end was a massive table attractively laid out with tea and scones and cakes. Seated at the table it was possible to look out on the sheepyards and outbuildings, and

Bridget saw Gareth striding towards the back door. Oh yes, there was no doubt that it was the same swift, purposeful stride, and the same lean well-muscled body. Time seemed to cease for her as she moved into a feeling of numbness that was beyond shock.

'Kathy, where's your little boy? Valinda, you'll adore him. He's quite irresistible.'

As Kathy moved away to pick up a happy baby boy who was playing by the sink, Valinda hissed under her breath, 'Oh, I can resist him all right. I hate kids. I wish I'd never said I'd come here!'

Bridget echoed that thought with her whole heart. The crucial test was coming. Lord, don't let him recognise me! It came to her suddenly that a new face, a new body and three extra inches would be no use unless she had a new personality as well. There must be no sign of the former timidity and shrinking back. She would have to be bold and confident. Easier said than done, but the first impression must be so far from the shy, short, fat little Bonnie that connecting them in Gareth's mind wouldn't even be a remote possibility.

Tense and expectant, she watched him enter and as she heard the firm deep voice speak, melted within.

'Good afternoon, everyone. I certainly know when to come home. That cuppa will be most welcome, Kathy darling, and scones with cream and raspberry jam are my special weakness. Now, Angel, introduce me to your visitors.'

Miss Curtis gave him a reproving but indulgent smile. 'Valinda Mason, my dear nephew's daughter, and her friend Bridget. Girls, this is Gareth Evans, my new manager.'

His smile had lost none of its charm, as he greeted
them, then bent to scoop up young Matthew on to
his knee as he sat down. 'You and I will have to
stick together, man. All these gorgeous women and
we two are the only able-bodied males present. We
could almost be described as an endangered species.'

All the anger and resentment was washed from
Valinda's face as if by magic. 'I'm sure you'll cope
adequately, Gareth.'

He took a sip of tea, then bit into a fresh scone
with obvious relish, and grinned at her. 'Only if
you're on my side, Valinda.'

'I'd like that. I always like to be on the winning
team.' Her eyes were alight with mischief. 'Why do
you call Aunt Grace Angel?'

'Who else would be guarding the gates of Paradise
Peaks?'

'Ridiculous boy!' Miss Curtis tried to look severe
and failed.

Bridget started to seethe a little. He had not
changed, sitting there with easy assurance and confidence, charming the whole company without the
slightest effort. Even the baby was snuggled up to
him with absolute contentment, and Kelly leaned
against his knee lovingly. Of course she'd known he'd
make a wonderful father, but did he have to look so
smug and self-satisfied!

Gareth glanced around the table. 'And where's
the dragon your father sent to guard you, Valinda?
He assured me he had a fierce and utterly competent
old maid schoolmistress, to play bird-dog with you.
Don't tell me, on your way here a handsome prince
saw your awful fate and drew a sword and slew her
with commendable swiftness. I'll have another scone
on the strength of his forethought. What we don't

need most is a crabbed and neurotic old maid causing problems at Paradise.'

As Valinda's laugh rang out, Bridget pushed back
her chair and walked to the head of the table to
where Gareth sat.

'I'm the dragon. Would you prefer me to breathe
fire or just roar, so that you can identify me more
easily?'

The last rays of the westering sun outlined her
slim, utterly feminine figure and turned her carefully
coiled hair into a halo of shining gold. Like an
avenging angel she glared at him, her temper adding
startling brilliance to her greeny-gold eyes, and the
flare of colour in her cheeks making her more vital
and attractive than she could possibly have believed.

Startled, Gareth put Matthew on the floor and
straightened up. 'Forgive me, I seem to have
dropped a real clanger. You're the very nicest
dragon I've ever met. No, I'm totally wrong, you're
not a dragon, but a delightful fairy godmother.
We're very fortunate to . . .'

'Sorry, Mr Evans, flattery or fantasy have relatively little effect on me, so I advise you to keep
your charm for your wife and children, and the more
susceptible members of the household.'

With a swirl of her softly pleated apricot dress,
Bridget turned and stalked to the door, then paused.
'When you've finished your afternoon tea, Mrs
Evans, I'd be grateful if you would show me to my
room. Valinda has a lot of work to get through in
the next six weeks, and I'd like to get her study programme set out tonight so she can make a start first
thing in the morning.'

She walked out to the Morris and started to
unload with unnecessary vigour. Old maid—

dragon—handsome prince—if anyone needed slaying it was Gareth Evans! She jumped as she heard him speak.

'Miss Marlow, I do humbly apologise for my stupid nonsense in the kitchen. I realise that your position . . .'

'Has been made far more difficult, by your facetious remarks. I'm sorry you don't approve of Mr Mason's choice, but your opinion of me is inconsequential. I'll do my job to the best of my ability. Mr Mason said I could count on you, and find you a tower of strength. However, he did say he'd never met you, so he may be forgiven for his mistake.'

'I've said I'm sorry. You can't hold one silly remark against me. I'll give you any support I can, that's a promise. Here, give me that box of books, it's too heavy for you.'

'I'm quite capable of carrying a box of books.' Bridget said angrily. 'I did ask that your wife would show us to our rooms.'

Gareth grinned. 'You'll be waiting a long time. I haven't got a wife.'

Bridget stared. 'But Kathy, and the children . . .'

He took the box from her unresisting hands. 'I'm not the only one to jump to a wrong conclusion this afternoon. Kathy is a widow, and was sent here by Miss Curtis's lawyer to take the place of Jess. You'll get us all sorted out soon enough.'

'Don't patronise me! At least it's not my style to make derogatory statements about people I've never met.' Bridget knew that was definitely an unfair thing to say, but she felt like being unfair. He wasn't married. All these years, her picture of him with a loving wife by his side and little children about him was all wrong. Here he was, heartwhole and fancy-free and, she had to admit, even more attractive than she remembered. She was furious, and what was worse, she had no idea why she was so angry.

She carried two of the lighter cases upstairs behind him, still feeling illogically upset.

'Here's your bedroom, Miss Marlow. Now I'll show you Valinda's. Miss Curtis is directly opposite you, and I sleep at the far end of the passage. Each room has its own bathroom, put in at enormous expense a few years ago, I might add.'

'How pleasant,' Bridget remarked, gathering from his tone that he disapproved of the renovations.

'Pleasant perhaps, but the project almost crippled the station financially. Thousands of dollars wasted on useless extravagance in the house and the land crying out for fencing and fertiliser.'

Gareth had turned at the entrance to the next room and faced her as he spoke. Bridget met his eyes coolly. 'It's Miss Curtis's property, so I presume she can indulge herself if she so wishes. I think you're making a huge fuss about putting in a bathroom or two. Lots of homes have private bathrooms in the bedrooms today.'

'In one or two rooms, perhaps. She had ten bathrooms put in, with only herself and a married couple living here.' His mouth tightened. 'I was stupid to expect you to understand, but when you admire the ballroom and reception room, just think how much it cost to paper those walls at over a hundred dollars a roll, then walk over to the sheepyards and inspect the woolshed with its shocking deterioration, so bad that respectable shearing gangs refuse to work here. Then you'll comprehend something of the problem facing Paradise Peaks.' He flung open the door and Bridget followed him into a fascinating bedroom, the walls covered in a stunning paper of wildflowers on a raw-silk-look background. The theme was carried through to the deeply flounced matching bedspread and echoed in a tiny, delicate arrangement on the windowsill. The luxurious lilac carpet and curtains added a certain delicate feminine touch to the room. The warm, glowing tones of the furniture spoke of a more gracious era. Nothing was overlooked in the interests of beauty and comfort.

Bridget walked to the desk at the east end of the room, and gazed down the wild and beautiful valley, and on to the grandeur of the surrounding mountains. 'There's a lake—oh, what a gem!'

'You can see the west arm of Lake Trident. Do you think Valinda can study here?'

'I think she'll love it. Why, it's larger than my whole flat!' She looked at the desk with angle-poise lights, the two deep-purple velvet chairs on either side of a small ornate fireplace and the small occasional table, the plentiful bookshelves, and a wee nook with coffee-making facilities. At the opposite end was a well appointed bathroom.

'Are all the rooms as gorgeous as this, Mr Evans?' she asked.

'Every damned one. Your room is in apricot tones. The wallpaper is textured linen with large bunches of flowers embroidered over it, and my room has the masculine touch—houndstooth checked paper called, I believe, Baskerville.'

'How appropriate,' Bridget murmured.

'You may find it amusing, but if the sinful waste of money had been stopped and channelled into the land instead, Miss Curtis could be living very comfortably now, not facing bankruptcy as she is.'

'You're exaggerating, of course,' Bridget replied.

'Valinda said her people were one of the first families to take up land here. You're just trying to get me on your side to bully that sweet old lady. Well, I won't be on your side, Mr Evans.'

His mouth twitched, 'I'm sure you'd make a stimulating adversary in different circumstances, but in the present situation you're going to need all the backing you can get to keep that young lady's nose to the grindstone. Why not admit we both made mistakes?'

'Mine was understandable. You picked up the baby, and called Kathy "darling".'

His grin was wicked. 'Because Kathy is a darling, as you'll find out. But if you're feeling neglected, I'll call you "darling" any time you like.'

'That will not be necessary,' Bridget replied sharply.

'Right, we'll dispense with the "darling" in the meantime. But if you'll drop the Mr Evans touch, I'll call you Bridget. We're a very friendly household here, and if you're going to take me head-on each time we meet, life will sour for everyone. I'd like to be friends with you, Bridget.'

'I'm prepared to call you Gareth, but I choose my friends a little more carefully than you do. I'll call a truce, if you agree. But I must ask you to refrain from encouraging Valinda to look on me as a warder. Do you realise that if she doesn't complete her lessons and get a decent report from the Correspondence School, the magistrate could well send her to a corrective school when she next appears before him?'

'I've already told her father I'll help you in any way I can. You can count on me, Bridget. I'll send Valinda up to you. See you at dinner.'

She watched his long lithe figure stride towards

the stairs, and went quickly to her room to recover herself before Valinda joined her. Her room was equally sumptuous and as delightfully furnished as the other one. It must have cost a fortune. She hung her few clothes in the wall-to-wall mirrored ward-robe and hoped she would find them again.

She turned towards the door as she heard Valinda running up the stairs. She was still a little troubled by the brightness in her eyes, and the soft glow in her cheeks ... it was just the excitement of having come through a tough situation with flying colours. But she would have to watch herself.

'Hey, Bridget!' Valinda burst into the room. 'Are you okay? I'm sorry Gareth upset you. He didn't mean to ... in a way it was a compliment that he didn't recognise you as my bodyguard.' She threw herself on the bed. 'Isn't he fantastic! So-o-o-o good-looking! Oh, I'm glad I came. I feel different already—free, you know. And he's not married. He'll do me. I'll need a little light relief to lift me up if I'm buried in swot all day. Or do your fancy him?'

Bridget snorted, 'I do not! He's all yours and wel-come, but I'd say you'll face some pretty strong competition from Kathy and the kids. Anyway, he's too old for you. Come along and we'll work out a schedule for you.'

'Phooey! Age is nothing today. Most men are at-tracted to young, sweet innocent things—makes them feel all masculine and protective. You watch!'

'And do you qualify as a sweet young innocent, Valinda?' asked Bridget drily.

'Well, I'm young, and I can be very sweet, for the right person, so two out of three isn't bad.' Valinda jumped off the bed and skipped ahead of Bridget down the passage and into her room. 'Almost palatial, isn't it? Dad went absolutely berserk when he found out what Aunt Grace had done, but she said she didn't have long to live and she wanted to leave something lovely behind her.'

'Was she talking generally or . . .'

'Two years ago the doctor gave her only a few months to live, and she looked awful, then suddenly she got this renovating bug and a new lease of life. Now she just *fills* the house with flowers, too—she's always had green fingers. Dad says she'll outlast him, but I know he's worried about her. She's a sweetie, and says she knows she's living on borrowed time, but she's going to enjoy every minute of it, and we're not to talk about it.'

Bridget helped Valinda unpack and plan out her timetable. 'Do you want me to stay with you during the day, Valinda? Or do you prefer to work on your own?'

'You mean I get a choice?'

'Certainly. Remember this is your own idea. I'm willing to help you, although your maths and physics are beyond me. You have two very good reasons for making a successful attempt on the exam, so I expect you to act responsibly about the amount of work you do.'

Valinda's pretty face tightened. 'I'm doing it for one reason, and one reason only. It's for Jody, so you needn't think you'll have to crack the whip. And I'll work on my own, if you don't mind. I'll shout if I need you.'

'Is that a promise?'

Valinda nodded, then pushed aside her books and took out a writing pad and ballpoint pen, 'Dinner will be in an hour, I'll knock on your door. I've got a letter to write first . . . to Jody's parents. After you left last night I thought about how sad they'll be without her. They're real parents, and I must have hurt them by the way I acted at the funeral. They deserve some sort of explanation.'

'I'm glad you want to do that,' said Bridget. 'It won't be an easy letter to write, but they'll really appreciate it.' As Bridget watched, Valinda's face crumpled and all the confidence and sophistication was stripped bare, leaving her young face stark with pain.

'Why do you bother with me?' Her voice was harsh. 'I'm worth nothing. The only decent thing in my life was Jody. Oh, God, I miss her so!' She leaned forward on the desk, covering her face with her hands, trying to hide the tears she could not control.

Bridget moved swiftly to put her arm around her, compassion flooding her heart. 'It's all right, Valinda. It will be all right. Why do I bother? Because I love you. You're precious and dear, and infinitely valuable . . .'

Valinda quietened after a few minutes, then muttered, 'Rubbish, muck metal, scrap metal— that's me. You're just soft—soft and stupid. You should have left me on the scrapheap. That's where I belong. I'll never make it back, and I don't want to. It's all uphill. Going down is easier.'

Bridget stepped away, wishing with all her heart that she had gained more experience before she tried to help.

'What a pity Jody was such a poor judge of character,' she said coldly.

Valinda's head came up, her blue eyes blazing. 'She was not! That's a rotten thing to say. Jody really knew people, what made them tick. I'd stake my life on her judgment. Why . . . why, she knew what was under your mask. She liked you.'

Bridget grinned, 'And she loved you. Can you imagine Jody throwing her friendship away on someone who could only be described as muck metal? She knew pure gold when she saw it. Mind you, I'd say there's a considerable amount of polishing to be done before others can see it shining.' She walked towards the door, then some instinct warned her and she turned just in time to duck a furiously accurate cushion hurling in her direction. She picked it up after it thudded against the wall, and tossed it back to Valinda with another grin. 'That's much better. Don't forget to call me on your way down.'

Back in her own room, Bridget scribbled a hurried note to her father pleading for his advice and guidance. She tried to be as accurate in her detail as possible, to give him an exact description of Valinda, and of her swift changes of behaviour. Should she be more strict or more lenient? But while she fully covered Valinda's problems, she carefully avoided mentioning her own. She did not want her father's loving advice. She knew his theory about God always bringing you back to face the same problem over and over again until you learned the lesson He was trying to teach you, and learned also to face your fear and overcome it.

Well, she would have to face Gareth, but only because there was no way out, and she had already learned her lesson . . . not to trust him. But conquering her fear, that was much more difficult to achieve. One fear was that Gareth would suddenly have something trigger his memory—a look or a gesture, or an expression, and he'd know that she was Bonnie Marlow, the poor lovesick teenager who had adored him four years ago. The other fear was much worse to contemplate, that some look or gesture of his would trigger off the same response in her heart that had been there four years ago. She must keep as far away from him as she could without causing comment, be ever alert when speaking to him, and present, always, an air of complete indifference and unconcern.

It sounded easy, but she knew it wouldn't be. She was fully aware of heightened colour in her cheeks and the added sparkle in her eyes as she hastily washed and retouched her make-up. She tried to tell herself it was just the challenge of the situation, but that did not account for the rapid beat of her heart when Valinda knocked on the door, or the wobbly feeling in her legs as she followed her down the curving staircase.

Kathy greeted them warmly, and Kelly looked adorable in a green full-length nightie trimmed with lace. She ran over to take Bridget's hand.

'I'm allowed to sit by you.' Her bright face was shining. 'Matthew's in bed. He's only little.'

'Don't let her make a nuisance of herself, Bridget.' Kathy warned. 'She'll monopolise you.'

'I couldn't think of anything nicer.' Bridget bent down and picked up Kelly. 'She's enchanting.'

'She can be when it suits her. Put your dressing-gown on, Kelly.'

'Doan hassle me, Mum.'

'Where's your dressing-gown, Kelly?' Bridget asked, firmly controlling her desire to laugh. 'Let me help you put it on.'

Valinda had gone straight to Gareth and the two of them were chatting like old friends. Bridget was deeply grateful to have something to do to save her from having to join them.

'I'm a big girl, aren't I?' Kelly demanded.

'Yes, you are. Put your arm in here.'

'You're big too.' It was obviously meant to be a high compliment.

'Thank you.' Bridget's smile deepened.

'You've got a nice hole in your face.' Kelly's small hand reached out to touch the clearly defined dimple.

'Kelly, don't make personal remarks like that,' Kathy scolded. 'Oh, I'm sorry, Bridget. She is a terrible child.'

'Don't worry. She probably hasn't met someone with a dimple before. May I help you serve dinner?'

Kathy smiled, 'You're very understanding. In church last month she suddenly announced in a loud, carrying voice "He's got no hair!" I nearly died, and when I tried to hush her, she said it even louder. Thank goodness the Vicar had a sense of humour. I have served the dinner, but you can carry it across to the table if you don't mind. It's always a battle at this time of night to get the children bathed and fed, put Matthew down and serve dinner.'

'Call on me any time, I'd love to help. I'm used to small children, and I'll probably have quite a bit of time on my hands.'

Gareth obviously overheard the last part of her conversation as they walked to the table, because he looked directly at her. 'Why will you have plenty of time on your hands?'

'Because Valinda prefers to study alone.' Bridget gave him a cool glance, then placed the plates where Kathy indicated.

'Can you ride?' Gareth shot the question at her.

She caught her breath sharply. Didn't he remember teaching her to ride? How stupid she was to

feel hurt because he didn't. 'A little. I rode for a
while, years ago. I was never very good.'

Thankfully she took her place. Miss Curtis sat at
one end of the table and Gareth at the other. Just as
they took their seats, two men came through the kitchen door and with hasty apologies took their places
opposite Bridget.

Gareth turned to Valinda. 'Meet Doug Courtenay
and Jamie Barclay, Valinda. Doug prefers the agri-
cultural work and Jamie the stock work. Boys, this is
Valinda Mason, Miss Curtis's niece, and across the
table from you is her friend Bridget Marlow.'

They were both tanned, smiling men. Doug, being
about Gareth's age, was fair with blue eyes and a
beard, and Jamie was younger with a shock of dark
hair and intelligent grey eyes. They both ack-
nowledged the introductions and became intent on
their meals.

As the meal finished and they reached the coffee
stage, Gareth turned his attention to Bridget again.
'I'm glad you can ride. We can do with some help.'

Bridget stared. 'Sorry, but I came here to supervise
Valinda's work.'

'We're massively understaffed here, I can't afford
to have someone sitting around with nothing to do,'
he said firmly. 'It will be good for you to be outside
. . . healthy in the fresh air . . . invigorating. You'll
only get in Kathy's hair hanging around the house.
You could get fat and unattractive and bored.'

Bridget's eyes flashed. Was he just pretending not
to recognise her? That mention of fat and unattractive sounded too much of a coincidence. 'I
won't do it! You can't make me.'

Miss Curtis tilted her head slightly to one side like
an interested bird. 'Don't be too hasty, Bridget. You

could quite enjoy being out on the station. Disregard what Gareth said about your attractive figure. I can tell you're the thoroughbred type, weight will never be your problem.'

'And my weight will never be Gareth's problem either,' Bridget fumed. 'I resent the implication that there'd be friction between Kathy and me if I stayed about the house. That's patently ridiculous. This is a huge house, and Kathy has two young children, plus having to cook for two extra now. I'm sure she could do with some help. Let's leave it up to her.'

'You fail to understand, Bridget, that I'm in full control of the staff on Paradise Peaks,' said Gareth. 'Angel here has a strict and unbreakable limit on how many I can employ, and as she's the owner, I have to accept her restrictions ... for the moment, but what is here I'll use. And I intend to use you.'

'Mr Mason pays my salary, not the station. I'll ring him.'

Gareth smiled. 'You do that. If he wants his daughter to study here ...'

Bridget was furious, 'Are you threatening me? How dare you!'

His smile broadened. 'Not threatening you, Bridget. But I've been having a talk to Valinda, and she'd love to come out and help. She's a good rider and would be a most acceptable addition to the team, without doubt much more useful than yourself. The decision is up to you ...'

'You'd actually jeopardise Valinda's future to get your own way?'

'Not me. That's why I suggested that you come with us. It's your choice.'

Miss Curtis laughed, 'He's a mean negotiator, Bridget.'

'He's despicable!' Bridget could hardly get the words out. She couldn't go out with him. She intended to avoid him. She glanced at Valinda, and knew by the impudent grin that Valinda was enjoying her predicament. The girl needed a good smacking. 'I'll ring Mr Mason tonight.'

Valinda giggled and lifted Gareth's hand above his head. 'The winner! Dad will back you, Gareth, he hates wasted labour. And I really don't think he'd approve of my being outside all day and trying to do my school work at night.'

Bridget was beaten and she knew it. She didn't feel like giving in gracefully. She rarely felt the need to swear, but at this moment she could think of several colourful expletives that would cover the situation. How could she ever have thought Gareth Evans charming? He was a brute!

'Whacko! We'll have the prettiest musterer in the high country riding with us.' Jamie's grey eyes held unexpected sympathy.

'Thank you, Jamie, It'll be a pleasure to ride with *you*.' Bridget smiled warmly at him. 'That's if I can still ride. It's been years.'

'I'll choose your horse, Bridget. I know just the right one—a real rocking chair. We'll have fun. Trust me.'

'I will indeed.' Bridget flicked a disdainful look at Gareth before turning to Kathy. 'May I help you with the dishes?'

'If you're not too tired, I'd be most grateful. We do have an automatic dishwasher, but it will give us a chance to get to know each other.'

Bridget's heart warmed to the friendly acceptance. She'd need friends if Gareth and Valinda were ganging up together.

'Valinda tells me that this isn't your first experience on a high country station?' Gareth interrupted. He made it a question.

'I don't believe Valinda has very much knowledge of my past to share with you,' Bridget answered curtly as she started to clear the table.

'Have you been on a station before?' Gareth demanded.

'Yes.'

'I've been about a bit, so have Doug and Jamie. Perhaps we've also been where you stayed, or close to it. We could maybe share a few memories.' His tone was pleasant, almost conciliatory, as if he was trying to mend fences.

'My memories are my own, and I have no intention of sharing them.' Bridget felt wretched about having to speak so rudely when Jamie and Doug had turned expectantly at the door to hear her answer. She didn't at all mind being rude to Gareth. In fact, it was a distinct pleasure.

'Are you gwumpy?' Kelly's small face was troubled.

Bridget swooped down to lift her up for a hug. 'Not with *you*, darling.'

'Goodnight, all,' Doug and Jamie called before leaving, and as Bridget turned to reply she got an encouraging wink from Jamie. She was so glad she had not offended him.

Kelly snuggled in. 'Can I help you with the dishes?'

'She'll slow you up,' Kathy warned.

'I'm in no hurry,' Bridget replied comfortably. 'If you've got something else to do, Kelly and I will pace each other.'

'Well, I would like to get on with the ironing if

you really mean that.' Kathy smiled happily as she brought out the ironing board. 'It's going to be just great having someone nearly my own age here.'

'Exactly my sentiments. I feel as if I've bitten off a little bit more than I can chew, taking on Valinda, and I was so nervous on my way out wondering how we'd fit in with the household.'

Kathy attacked the ironing with brisk efficency and, by the time Bridget and Kelly had tidied up, she had nearly completed her work.

'What's next on the agenda?' Bridget asked.

'Wouldn't you rather go through to the lounge with the others?' Kathy asked. 'I feel awful making you work the first night . . .'

'I'd much rather be here,' Bridget replied honestly.

'Well, if you're sure. Kelly seems to have taken to you really well. Would you like to put her to bed? Would you like that, Kelly?'

'Yes. Bwidget is my fwiend.'

Bridget caught the dainty wee girl in her arms. 'That's for sure. Now, what's the routine?'

'Kelly is to go to the toilet first. She'll show you where the bathroom is. Then prayers, then if you don't mind reading her a story. By that time I'll have all this away, and will set the table ready for the morning, and we'll share a cuppa.'

When Kelly fell asleep half way through 'The Three Bears' Bridget went out to join Kathy. 'That's a nice little flat you've got there,' she commented. 'Very convenient.'

'Yes. I'm so grateful to Gareth for thinking of me when he came here. I was in a State unit in town, hating every minute of it. It's so good to be back in the country. But Gareth's like that. He was a friend of my husband, and has kept an eye out for us ever since Brent died.'

'How long ago, Kathy?'

'Fourteen months. He never even saw Matthew.' Kathy's lip quivered. 'Seems only like yesterday, sometimes, then at other times it feels I've been on my own so long. Still, I've got the kids, so I shouldn't grizzle.'

'Were you very happy, you and your husband?' asked Bridget.

'We were to start off with, then Brent started drinking and getting around with the single guys on the station, and things got a bit grim. But we would have worked it out. I loved him very much, and he loved me in his own way.'

'I'm sure he did,' Bridget thought it would be hard to imagine anyone not loving Kathy. Gareth? Was that why he had got her the position? She felt like screaming because her mind had winged its way straight to him. He was *nothing* to her.

Kathy brightened suddenly. 'I'm very, very lucky to be here, and you must forgive me rambling on about my own worries. Tell me, how did you get involved with Valinda? And can you tell me what her problem is? I mean, I wouldn't want to pry if it's confidential. I can see she's a lovely girl, but I can also see she's been through something very tough—there's a brittleness about her. I'd love to help her if I could.'

'You probably can, just by showing her you don't condemn her. And like you, she's lost someone she loved very dearly, and she blames herself for her friend's death. I don't see why you shouldn't know her story. The papers got hold of it, so it became public, anyway.'

As Bridget told her of Valinda's pain, Kathy's soft heart was touched and she could not help crying. 'Oh, poor kid! I'm glad you told me. It will help me to show a little understanding if she acts up sometimes. I know what I was like—I wanted to hit out and hurt someone in sheer frustration. What a worry for her parents! They must be really grateful to you. I don't envy you. But you can count on me, any time, Bridget.'

'I hoped you'd say that,' smiled Bridget.

Kathy looked at the clock. 'Wow! It's time I took in the supper. I have to get to bed fairly early, otherwise I'd never make it in time for breakfast. Especially if the kids have a disturbed night.'

Bridget helped her prepare the tray, but shook her head when Kathy suggested popping an extra cup on for her.

'No, thanks. I'm just about awash anyway, and I have no desire to have another encounter with Gareth. Remember, I have to be up early too.'

Kathy's small face looked troubled. 'I'm sorry you and Gareth seem to strike sparks off each other. He's just the greatest guy, really he is.'

'Spare me the details, please. Just remember, one man's meat is another man's poison. That way we'll be friends.'

'You mustn't blame him for making you go out on the farm,' Kathy persisted. 'Not that he doesn't need your help, but I was sitting up that end of the table, and I heard Valinda priming him up . . . really she did.'

Bridget's lips tightened. 'Thanks. I had a feeling she was up to something, but he didn't need to take her advice. Goodnight, Kathy, see you in the morning.'

Bridget showered in her elegant private bathroom, enjoying the tasteful appointments all the more because Gareth had shown his disapproval of the luxury. Back in her room she drew her robe more closely about her slender shape and wandered to the window as she brushed her hair in long strokes. How beautiful the valley showed in the moonlight, dark-shadowed and mysterious on the tussock plains and beyond, to the towering rugged tops still coated with winter snows, remote and cruel, yet beautiful surpassing description. Tomorrow she would ride beside Gareth again. The thought sent the blood pounding through her veins and she despised herself for the well-spring of joy that bubbled up within her, but she was unable to quell it.

She would never sleep. But she had to try. She switched off the light and slid between the sheets. So many impressions crowded on her mind—Jody, Valinda, the magistrate, Miss Curtis, Kathy and the children, the men, Jamie's swift acceptance of her, and the wild, wild beautiful land, and the stars which had canopied the sky, somehow larger, clearer, more brilliant than she had ever seen. Jody had been correct in her diagnosis ... she had kept her emotions in cold storage, deep-frozen to protect herself, and this pain she was feeling was the stirring of desires and hopes that she had long buried.

She turned over and hid her face in the pillow, trying to blot out the image of Gareth's smiling face, his teeth startlingly white against the dark mahogany-tanned skin. His deep brown eyes which could be so tender, and at other times full of fire and fury, his body—lithe and sinewy, and virile. It wasn't fair, it just wasn't fair. She had put him out of her life, and that had taken four years. She had put away all thought of romance, of marriage, of children, because of one man, and now she was being forced to share a house with him, to confront him and resist him every day for the next six weeks.

But resist him she would, to her last breath, she vowed to herself. She was older now, and stronger, and aware of the danger. She would give him nothing, not friendship or even common courtesy, and she would crush down these emotions that were stirring within her, crush them ruthlessly, and retreat back into the carefully controlled remote and objective view of life which had sustained her. She had nothing to fear. Gareth was only a man.

CHAPTER FIVE

'RISE and shine!' Gareth's voice woke Bridget from her restless sleep. He pounded on the door just to make sure she was awake, then she heard him walk away towards the stairs.

She launched out of bed and hastily washed and dressed in her comfortable jeans and casual shirt, then quickly braided her hair into one thick golden plait. She pulled on a pair of thick socks and tied her low-heeled brogue shoes with shaking hands, chose a heavy cable-knit jersey, then hurried down the stairs and out to the kitchen.

Kelly greeted her rapturously, and Matthew staggered drunkenly towards her with a devastating grin on his baby face. Bridget bent to kiss them before saying a general good morning to the men and Kathy, who were seated at the table. She slid into her place and helped herself to fruit and cereal, refusing the offer of a cooked breakfast.

'You'd better stoke up, Bridget,' Gareth remarked 'We won't be back here till nightfall. Kathy has packed our lunch.'

Bridget did not reply. How on earth would she survive being on a horse all day?

'You'll do fine,' Jamie was grinning across the table at her as if he had read her mind. 'And if you don't, we'll bury you out there where the wind blows free. You couldn't have a better resting place.'

'Jamie!' Kathy glared at him for a moment, then giggled, 'A bit like that poem I learned in school,

"Bury me in a foreign land something-or-other will remain for ever England."'

Bridget gave her a reproachful look. 'If you're going to quote poetry over my dead body, you could at least get it right—it is "If I should die, think only this of me: that there's some corner of a foreign field that is forever England."'

'Enough talk,' Gareth said sharply. 'We've got plenty to get through today.'

Silence fell, except for Kelly chatting to her doll, until Valinda came through the door, radiating goodwill and cheerfulness.

' 'Morning, all! I sure wish I was going with you. It's going to be a glorious day, I just saw the sun rising over Peter, Paul and Luke—fabulous!' She patted Gareth on the shoulder before sitting down beside him. 'Go on, Gareth, invite me, then stand back and watch me succumb.'

Bridget watched his face soften into a smile as he gazed at Valinda's enchanting smile. 'The temptation is all mine, Valinda. Tell you what—I'll leave a horse in the yard, and when you've finished your studies, saddle up and join us. I'll look forward to it all day.'

'You're on!' Valinda responded jubilantly.

Bridget followed the men across to the yards and leaned against the rail as she watched them saddle up, trying to pick her own horse. Jamie came towards her leading a bay mare with a white blaze down its face.

'Let me introduce you to Nadia, she's a sweetie. Look at her gentle eye, and her mouth is soft as silk. Here, do you want a leg up?'

'No, thanks, I'll manage,' Bridget muttered grimly. Perhaps Nadia could be induced to buck her off here and break her bones, then she wouldn't have to go. She gathered up the reins and planted her foot firmly in the stirrup, and was surprised how fluidly she mounted. Maybe it wasn't going to be all bad.

'Here, let me adjust the stirrups for you. They need to be a bit shorter.' Jamie quickly altered them. 'I'll get my nag, and we'll be off.'

Bridget sat in the early morning sunlight, watching the men loose the dogs and wishing she could smile at their excited cavorting, but smiling was beyond her. She saw Doug drive off with the tractor and then the men mounted up, Jamie also riding a bay horse and Gareth on a big black gelding that reared and pranced like a circus ballerina. Showing off, thought Bridget sourly, then he rode off down the lane without even sparing her a glance. She urged Nadia along and followed him, and Jamie caught up and rode beside her.

'Stir her along a bit,' he advised.

'You're joking,' Bridget hissed. 'I'm barely staying aboard at a slow walk.'

'You can do better than that,' he said with a grin, and leaned over and gave Nadia a sharp slap on the rump, then kicked his own horse into a canter.

Nadia leaped forward like a racehorse at the starting gate, and Bridget clung desperately to keep her balance, then relaxed as the horse took up an easy swinging stride. After a few minutes Bridget smiled. It was wonderful, exhilarating, divine. Perhaps riding a horse was like learning to ride a bike—you never quite forgot how to do it. She leaned forward to pat Nadia. 'You wee beauty, you lovely wee horse.'

As if she had been waiting for encouragement,

Nadia changed gear and took off like a rocket, sweeping past Jamie and gathering in Gareth and his big black horse and then outdistancing the dogs, who were caught by surprise. Bridget let her run for a distance, then pulled her in and sat waiting for the men to catch up.

'If you run your horse like that first thing, she'll be gutted by the time the end of the day comes.' Gareth spoke disapprovingly.

But Bridget grinned unrepentantly. It had been a fine gallop, and she felt miles more confident. What a morning, oh, what a wonderful day! She turned Nadia alongside Jamie, loving his admiring look. At least *he* shared her pleasure.

'Wooee! I thought you said you hadn't ridden for years,' Jamie remarked, his grey eyes sparkling. 'That was some performance. You're a natural. I can see you winning the Queen of the Rodeo without even trying.'

'What does that entail? Not falling off your horse in the first ten minutes? If that's all there is to it I might qualify.'

'No, there's a hell of a lot more to it than that, but you've got the makings. You get points for riding, points for your horse and points for your appearance. You've got a great figure. I can just see you all togged out in Western gear, stetson and all, with your looks and that honey-blonde hair flying loose, and those long legs of yours, there wouldn't be another girl to touch you. I'll teach you to ride. How about it?'

Bridget's laughter rang out free and happy, making Gareth turn in his saddle and glance back. Something in his look made Bridget angry and she tossed her hair back, her eyes alight with mischief.

'As Valinda would say, "You're on". Do you ride in rodeos, Jamie?'

'I live for them. Some day I'll make it to the U.S.A. into the big time. That's my dream, hook your star to my wagon and I'll take you with me.'

'Thanks for the offer, but I'll wait and see how appealing it is when the day is over.' The mountain air was as heady as wine and, for no reason she could think of, Bridget's spirits soared high and higher yet as her gaze lifted to the amethyst hills. The warm, gentle wind caressed her cheek and tugged at her hair, and suddenly she longed for a star to follow— her destiny. Unconsciously her eyes turned to watch Gareth riding ahead, with his straight back and the easy set of his shoulders, at one with his horse, blending into the landscape with such harmony that he almost seemed part of the majestic mountains and waving sea of golden-brown tussock, arrogant and free, yet remote and lonely.

As they rode nearer the lake, wild Paradise ducks winged their way across it and a skein of Canadian geese, which had been following the river, flew low over the tussock. The three arms of the lake were in full view now, a perfect trident, and blue waters sparkled in the warm morning air. Reeds and flax and native trees bordered the edges, giving it the setting of a fantastically crafted gem of great beauty hidden in the hollow of the hills, its surface catching and holding the reflection of the blue sky, and the lofty, snow-clad peaks.

Day after day for two weeks Bridget rode and worked with the men, and her fascination with the mountains and tussock plains did not diminish, but grew and expanded and stripped bare from her all the stiffness and cramped emotions, leaving her open to a torrent of new feelings. She was filled with a wild singing excitement and such joy as she had never before experienced. Days when her every vein, artery and muscle screamed out for rest from the punishment that was being meted out to them, had no power to dampen her joyful enthusiasm.

It wasn't being with Gareth, she was sure of that, although he was part of it. She laughed as she thought how she had intended to be aloof and distant with him, because he had apparently come to the self-same decision, and ignored her, except to dish out orders. It suited her just fine. She kept with Jamie mostly, and Gareth paired them off whenever the work permitted, as if he was glad to be away from her. She did everything he told her to, without question, from riding the hills and valleys to walking behind the mobs of sheep with Nadia's reins looped over her arm, with Joe, her dog, at her side, to taking care of the Spinning Jenny as they rolled out the miles of fencing wire for the solar electric fence unit.

Girl Friday, as Jamie called her, the last in the pecking order. Holding the staples as they hammered on the battens, taking messages from the job back to the house, and from the house out to the plane which was aerial sowing the fertilizer and grass seed, pushing the reluctant sheep through the rickety sheep yards, and Bridget loved every minute of it.

She loved Joe, the crazy little dog which had become attached to her, even though the men said he was a *sooner*, meaning he would sooner sleep than work. He was hairy and dark, like an animal out of Sesame Street, or a rag mat, but she defended him because he worked for her when all the other dogs just ignored her. As she sat in the tussock eating her lunch with the men, and listening to them talk, Joe lay at her feet with such a look of adoring bliss, she could not eat unless he shared her food.

The sun bleached her hair and tanned her skin to a glowing apricot, the exercise whittled her figure even slimmer, and she felt the satisfaction of reaching a new peak in physical fitness. In two weeks, Paradise Peaks had become her life and she could hardly bear to contemplate the end of her time here, an end which was inevitable. Part of her happiness was in the way Valinda had set into her study, and was turning out work well above any standard Bridget could have imagined. Another part was sharing Kelly and Matthew with Kathy, and coming to love and know them more each passing day.

Gareth was not rude to her, nor could she say he was indifferent, more like watchful and wary . . . and expectant. Sometimes when she was laughing with Jamie or the children, she would look up and catch him watching her, and his searching gaze would reach right into her heart and make her breath clot in her throat until he looked away.

Today being Saturday, Valinda had been out with them all day, and as they rode home Bridget watched her ride beside Gareth, knee to knee, sublimely sure of her reception. Sometimes Bridget wished she could approach him with the same easy manner, and have him smile and tease her as he did Kathy and Valinda, but that way was not for her. Far better to keep her distance, then when she left there would be no pain. Last time it had been like an amputation, and the healing had been so slow.

At the stables they busied themselves unsaddling and turning the horses out. Valinda caught up on Bridget as she walked to the house.

'Do you know the men are going in to town

tonight? They usually do on a Saturday night. A lot of people who work on other stations gather there and it's fun. Why don't you go too?'

'I haven't been invited, and even if I had it has no appeal, but I'll ask Kathy if she wants to go. I could babysit for her. It will do her good to go out.'

'I think you should go.' Valinda seemed annoyed. 'After all, you've been out with the men ever since you've been here. It's a way of wiping out any misunderstandings or grievances, have a few drinks, a few laughs and start the new week fresh.'

Bridget laughed, 'I am grateful for your thought for me, Valinda, but I've got no grievances or misunderstandings to clear away. I am extremely happy.'

Valinda gave her a curious stare. 'You really are, aren't you? Jody was right about you—that quiet just before the glory of the sunrise. You've got it now—a real high-velocity beauty, like someone catching fire. You're not the same person who came here with me.'

'Neither are you, Valinda.' Bridget parried the compliment, not believing it, but not wanting to become engrossed in any personal catechism.

'Tell you what,' said Valinda, 'I'll babysit, then you and Kathy can both go.'

'That's most generous of you, but I'm not going, because I don't want to go.'

'Well, if you don't go, I will,' Valinda flared angrily.

Bridget stopped. 'You can't have a night out at a pub—you're under age. Normally that wouldn't matter, you'd probably only get a reprimand and be sent out, but you can't afford to take chances. Be sensible. You know what the magistrate said—one wrong move . . .'

'You be sensible, then,' Valinda retorted. 'You go and I'll stay home. Gareth wants you to go, so does Jamie.'

'Did Gareth put you up to this?' Bridget stared at her disbelievingly.

'Not exactly. He just said it would be nice if you all went, but he reckoned you wouldn't, and I said that you would if it was put to you the right way.'

'Well, to save an argument, pretend that there isn't any right way, because I'm tired. Now, let's forget it.'

'I won't. Unless you go, I will, and it will be all your fault if I get picked up. If you cared about me at all . . .'

'I do care about you,' Bridget said firmly. 'I wouldn't be here if I didn't care about you a great deal, but I won't be manipulated either.'

Valinda twisted around, 'Well, it's your choice, I'm going back to tell Gareth I'm going with them.'

Bridget continued to walk towards the house, wondering how to cope with the problem, then she pushed it away from her mind. Gareth wasn't that silly. He'd see the situation for what it was. Kelly was waiting at the door.

'You've been a long time. I've been waiting for *since*!'

'Have you, darling? I'm sorry. For since is indeed a long time. Hello, Kathy. Valinda was just telling me the men are going in to Hanmer for the evening. Would you like a night out? I'll look after the kids— I'd love to. How about it?'

Kathy's face brightened, 'Why, I can't remember when I've been out on the loose. I'd love it, if you think you can cope.'

'With one hand tied behind my back,' Bridget boasted. 'The kids are used to me now. I'll hop up and shower, then take over dinner while you change.'

Kathy still looked a bit dubious. 'You're tired and I'm afraid Kelly has used up all her good for the day. She's been really scratchy this afternoon.'

'We'll manage,' Bridget assured her.

'I will, if you're sure. Have you heard Kelly's new expression? That's how I feel. I haven't been out for *since* . . . it will be fun.'

Bridget showered and changed, with Kelly's help, and returned to the kitchen to find the men had been even faster than her. Doug, Jamie and Gareth were freshly showered and looking remarkably attractive in their leisure shirts and casual slacks. Valinda was standing a little to one side with a sulky expression on her face.

Gareth spoke. 'You won't have to bother with dinner for us—we'll have a meal in town. Make a nice change for Kathy to eat someone else's cooking. How come you won't come with us? Valinda said she offered to babysit.'

'The children know me better than they do Valinda,' said Bridget. 'I think Kathy would be happier leaving them with me.'

'Did you ask her?' Gareth demanded.

'No, I didn't. I decided quite rashly, that I could please myself what I did with my free time.' Then, feeling a bit ashamed of her sharp reply, she added, 'Jamie has offered to take me for a ride on Sunday, up to Hell's Gate where the wild cattle are, and I wanted to get a good sleep tonight, so I wouldn't hold him up.'

Valinda brightened. 'Can I go, too?'

Relieved at her change in mood, Bridget answered her with a smile, 'I don't see why not, but you'll have to ask Jamie!'

'Why should I?'

'Because it's polite. He invited me . . .'

'And I'm not inviting you this time, Valinda,' Jamie said firmly. 'You can come next time, but tomorrow belongs to Bridget.'

Valinda glared at him, 'You can forget it. I wouldn't go with you if you asked me. Nor you, Gareth Evans, coming all high and mighty and refusing to let me go to the pub! I bet it will be dead boring anyway. To hell with the lot of you! I'm going to my room, and I don't want any dinner, so don't come in and disturb me, Bridget, if you know what's good for you!' She ran from the room, slamming the door viciously behind her.

Kathy came in just as Valinda rushed out. 'What's happened? Why was Valinda crying?'

Gareth looked upset. 'She wanted to go to Hanmer with us, but I told her she'd better not while this case is hanging fire. If Bridget had agreed to accept her very kind offer, this wouldn't have happened.'

'She's a spoilt little brat,' said Jamie. 'And I have no intention of having my Saturday night ruined by one of her tantrums, so I'm on my way. She's a complete scatterbrain, she's caused everyone a packet of trouble and I want nothing to do with her. I've seen her sort before, and that's why I didn't want to take her with us on Sunday. Goodnight, Bridget. I wish you were coming too, but I'm glad you didn't let her bluff you. I'll take my own jalopy.'

After they left Bridget was kept too busy with Miss

Curtis and the children to spare much thought for Valinda, much less go up to see her. She was still simmering at the fact that Gareth made it out to be her fault that the whole thing blew up. She was surprised at Jamie's attitude and, thinking back, she realised that he had been studied in his avoidance of any overtures from Valinda ever since they had arrived. Even the first night he had immediately championed Bridget. All the time the nagging thought in her mind was why Valinda had been so keen to send her with the men. Valinda wasn't that fond of the children—still, it must have been a blow to her pride to have Gareth pull rank on her, then Jamie refusing her the pleasure of the trip on Sunday. She made up her mind to speak to Jamie in the morning and see if he would change his mind and allow Valinda to ride with them—she had been so good, it was tragic that this upset had happened.

Kelly was overtired and took a lot of settling, and Matthew screamed every time Bridget tried to put him down. As soon as she lifted him he smiled angelically and snuggled his head under her chin. Sleep was the furthest thought from his mind. She carried him through to the lounge and he became engrossed, watching the TV from the vantage point of Miss Curtis's knee.

'He's young to be an addict,' Miss Curtis laughed, but as always she was charmed by his company.

'I'll leave him with you, if he's not a nuisance,' said Bridget, 'and go and do the dishes.'

Half an hour later she returned to find Matthew sound asleep and she scooped him up with a heartfelt sigh of relief.

'Valinda's lucky she didn't land him tonight. I don't know what got into him, he usually goes down like a lamb. I'll pop him in his bed, then go up and see Valinda. She may be feeling hungry by now. Then I'll bring your supper in.'

'Don't hurry, dear, you must be tired after the long day you've had. I really do admire the way you've made yourself useful here, and I'll tell my nephew so when he rings. He made a wise choice.'

Bridget tucked Matthew down, pulled the covers over Kelly, then hurried upstairs, hoping Valinda had regained her composure. She knocked lightly and, receiving no reply, opened the door quietly. There was no use waking her up if she really had gone to sleep.

The light was on and one glance sufficed to show there was no one in the room. A note propped against the pillow caught Bridget's attention and, filled with sudden apprehension, she snatched it up.

'I'm taking your car and am off to the bright lights. Nobody wants me here. Don't hold your breath waiting for me to come back.'

Bridget stared at it, too shocked to take in all the implications at once. How long had Valinda been gone? Maybe she could stop her. Down the stairs she raced and ran towards the car shed. The Morris was gone; Valinda must have taken the keys from her dressing table. Sick at heart, Bridget made her way slowly back to the house. She thought of all sorts of impossible schemes, like ringing Hanmer and asking Gareth to drive to the junction and stop Valinda, but she was probably miles past there already. The Valiant, Miss Curtis's car, was sitting there. Could she possibly borrow it and catch Valinda before she got to Christchurch? No, that was ridiculous. Valinda knew the route far better than she did, and she could not abandon the children. She had an obligation there too.

Perhaps Valinda would get half way there and realise what she was throwing away and return home. The thought was a pretty forlorn one. Valinda was well known for her ability to carry out the most far-fetched plans. There was no point in upsetting Miss Curtis yet; there would be plenty of time for that in the morning. She would make the supper and carry on as if all was normal, but the anxiety was eating into her and it would not be easy.

All the time she shared supper with Miss Curtis, Bridget tried to focus on the T.V. programme but she could not concentrate. Where would Valinda go? Back to the gang at that club house? What if the police had cause to go there again? Everything would be lost. She was a complete failure. And say Valinda was picked up driving the car? That was just as bad.

Perhaps Valinda was just trying to throw a scare into her. Well, she had succeeded admirably. And Bridget started blaming herself terribly, for not going to the hotel . . . at least Valinda would have been stuck with the children. Just because she could not bear to go out with Gareth—it had been a pretty poor excuse for dodging the invitation.

Miss Curtis sat up until after eleven and Bridget stayed to keep her company, hating the moment when she would be on her own and forced to live with her regrets. And she kept hoping against hope that she would hear a car go back up the rise, past the house.

Then, when Miss Curtis retired, she checked the children and wandered restlessly up the stairs to her room, on to Valinda's room, and back down the stairs to the kitchen. Unconsciously she was praying,

'Lord, you look after her, and bring her back safe and sound.'

As if in answer to her prayer she heard a car drive up to the car-shed and she went out the door in a flash, running so fast her feet hardly touched the ground. She couldn't wait to tell Valinda how glad she was to see her, to hug her and love her. Poor girl, she had had enough rejections without Gareth, Jamie and Bridget herself adding to the score.

The moon slipped behind a cloud just as she reached the shed and in the dark she collided heavily with a strong masculine figure. 'Gareth!' The wind was almost knocked from her body, and if his strong arms had not immediately encircled her, she would have fallen over. He was quick to hear the despair in her voice.

'Who were you expecting?' He sounded amused. 'I gather it wasn't me, but I'm not averse to having a pretty girl rush headlong into my arms. Such an eager welcome makes me glad I came home early.'

'Let me go!' Bridget spluttered furiously. 'Of course it wasn't you!'

'I'll let you go when you tell me who was supposed to be the recipient of such unbridled passion. But don't hurry, I must say I'm enjoying having the oh, so prim and proper Miss Marlow swooning in my manly embrace.'

'I am not swooning! It would take a bigger man than you to make me swoon!'

'Would it indeed? Rash words, young Bridget, but nevertheless I accept the challenge.'

Moonlight flooded the valley and she could see his face, his brown eyes alight with mischief, and she struggled frantically, knowing he was going to kiss her and part of her bitterly regretting her stupid bravado, and yet the other part of her singing a wild song of joy that he'd called her pretty and wanted to go on holding her.

Ignoring her struggles, he drew her closer and closer, then taking all the time in the world, with his right hand he lifted her chin, his lips covered hers and she knew again the glorious feeling of being swept on a flood tide of emotions that carried away all her carefully programmed responses, and, un-ashamed, she lifted her arms and slid them behind his head and pulled him nearer. His searching lips released and filled the long hidden desires and emptiness of years of longing. She would savour this one moment, treasure it, and if pain and sorrow followed she would accept them, because nothing could ever destroy the sweet surging joy of being in Gareth's arms again.

He put her away from him gently, his expression enigmatic. 'You're quite a surprise, young Bridget. Jamie is a lucky fellow.'

'I wasn't expecting Jamie,' Bridget replied in a low voice, her head lowered so that he would not see the love and tenderness she knew would be reflected in her eyes. 'It's Valinda. She's run away. She took my car and has gone back to Christchurch, and she believes that none of us wanted her here. I feel so ashamed that I didn't see her need. She's been through such a rough time, and I added to it, and now she's thrown away her only chance. I've failed her . . .'

'Rubbish! You're the one stable influence in her life, and she was just trying you out. She's told me of your courage and your kindness when she was in gaol, and she knows that few, if any, of her friends or relations would have barrelled in there and gone in to bat for her. Even if they had they would have lacked the sensitivity and discernment to get to the root cause of her turmoil. You made her face the fact of Jody's death, and you gave her an understanding of death that she could accept. You've got nothing to blame yourself for.'

'I thought you blamed me as well for not taking her offer to babysit.' Bridget lifted her eyes to search his for the reassurance she desperately needed.

Gareth grinned at her, 'I was annoyed because you wouldn't come with us and I let my disappointment show. Also, you put me in a corner where I had to refuse to take her, and I didn't enjoy the position, so I very meanly tried to put it all on to you. I'm sorry.'

Bridget had forgotten how honest he was. It was so much part of his character, which she had admired years ago, and yet she had forgotten it. Why did most men feel to admit to a mistake made them small, whereas, in her estimation, he was as tall as the amethyst hills?

'Thank you,' she said simply. 'Still, if I had gone I wouldn't have forced her to take this action.'

Gareth leaned forward and took her arm casually, as if there had been no difficulty in their relationship, as if there had been no shared kiss, and turned her towards the homestead.

'Let's go and have a cup of coffee, and talk this over.'

Relief flooded her whole being. He was not going to make capital of her more-than-generous response to his carelessly taken kiss, and she was so grateful. He was not going to laugh at her fears for Valinda, but was offering to share the load. She went with him gladly, and with singing heart hurried to put the kettle on and search the biscuit tins for his favourite biscuits. Later she would deal with her feelings, but just now she was too weak to keep her guard against his offer of friendship.

He had stirred up the embers of the fire and thrown on another log, and, as she came in with the tray, hurried to take it from her and place it on the occasional table. His smile held a new warmth, a new and exciting interest, but when she met the look in his eyes, she quickly dropped her gaze. Her heart throbbed within her, and the blood coursed through her body like a raging fever, as it came to her that this intimacy could, with the slightest encouragement from her, be extended to another captured moment of ecstasy. But she did not dare give that encouragement.

Tonight must be a small oasis in the desert of years of longing. To go further was to invite disaster, to invite a pain of parting that would be unendurable. That one kiss had stirred up a fire in her that could never be qenched, but it did not need to be stoked either.

'You were going to talk about Valinda.' Her voice was husky with the effort she was making to sound normal.

Gareth picked up her coffee mug and shifted his long, lean frame into a more comfortable position. 'Only to say, far from blaming yourself for refusing to be manipulated into going out for the night, you probably gained her respect. Sure she's angry now, but she'll get over that. Not enough people in her life have dared to say no, and mean it. We all need to learn that we can't have everything in life, and Valinda in particular has to know that just because people love her it doesn't mean she can bend and twist them for her own ends.'

Bridget looked at him in surprise. 'But what if she doesn't come back?'

He smiled reassuringly, 'She'll come back. You had faith in her character when you accepted charge of her. Have you lost that faith?'

'Of course not,' Bridget protested indignantly.

'Well, you'll just have to sit it out. I could offer to take you up to the city and help you run a search and rescue mission—that is, after Kathy and the boys get home—she'll love that. She likes a bit of drama, but I think if you wait patiently for her to come back, she'll turn up none the worse for wear. She's highly intelligent, and it's much better that she sorts herself out and returns of her own accord. Don't you agree with me?'

'Yes, oh yes, I do agree.' Bridget suddenly felt foolish for becoming so frantic, and knew that if Gareth had not come home early and talked to her she would have got worse, not better.

'What happened to the others?' she asked. 'Why did you come home early?'

He shrugged his shoulders and leaned forward for another biscuit. 'Perhaps the evening went sour on me because I missed your stimulating company. Or perhaps I was too tired to enjoy myself. Then I have to admit I was troubled about Valinda. Whatever the reason, I'm glad I did.'

His voice had a certain inflection that made Bridget colour a little with confusion. She said, nervously, 'I—I think I'll ring my father, Mr Mason said I could any time I needed advice, and it would help me to relax if he feels the same way as you.'

'Do you think he will?'

Bridget looked at him thoughtfully. 'Yes, somehow I think he will.'

'You think a lot of your father, don't you, Bridget?'

Bridget nodded, unable to speak, because it was almost as if he was asking did she think a lot of him. She wasn't prepared to answer that question, and hurriedly left the room.

When she returned, feeling soothed and loved as always by her father's voice, she found Gareth had washed the coffee mugs and put the biscuits away. He asked, 'Happier now?'

'Yes, I am. He said if I believed that God had the whole world in His hands, why should I not consider His love and protection sufficient for Valinda as it was for myself? Then he finished up by saying I should go to bed and get a good night's sleep.'

Gareth hung up the tea-towel. 'A man of sound common sense. Let's go to bed, Bridget.' He roared with laughing at her expression. 'Sorry, I should have said, our respective beds.'

Angry at herself for blushing, Bridget replied, 'I've got to check on the children, and sit up for Kathy to come home.'

'Would you like me to keep you company?' He was closer now, the laughter barely hidden in his dark eyes.

She backed away, and was stopped abruptly by the sink bench. Her hands went out instinctively to ward him off. 'No, I prefer to wait on my own.'

Gareth caught her two hands in his. 'You're a complete mystery girl. I watch you so often laughing and joking with Jamie, playing with the children, in fact your attitude to every other member of the household is transparently open and honest and loving, but you're wary and on the defensive any time I speak to you. Are you afraid of me?'

Bridget's small chin lifted. 'I am *not!*'

He grinned, 'No, you're not, that's what puzzles me. You're as gutsy as they come. You ride that horse as if you were practising to lead the Charge of the Light Brigade, and you love it. I've been really pushing you to find a weak spot, to see when you'll cry quits, and I have to admit I haven't found any job that you won't throw your heart into—whether it's dangerous or boring, you'll go till you drop, then you come home here covered in dust or mud, shower and return to the kitchen looking fantastically feminine and put in another couple of hours helping Kathy, playing with the children, encouraging Valinda, and charming the rest of us mindless with your vitality and enthusiasm. Yet I know there's a barrier between us. Why, Bridget?'

She shrugged her shoulders. In the face of his complimentary remarks, and his own honesty, she felt horrible to be so unresponsive, but she dared not allow herself to be drawn into friendship with him. As she struggled to release her hands, he merely moved closer, imprisoning them in one strong, brown hand against his chest and leaving his right hand free.

'This is the reason I came home ahead of the others. I knew you'd have to stay with the children, and I thought if we could have a talk, maybe we could straighten things out between us.'

She refused to meet his eyes, staring grimly at the button of his open-necked casual shirt, terribly aware of his closeness, and her own weakness. Casually his hand caressed her hair, stroking the long silken length of it, pushing it away from her face behind her ears, then his finger gently outlined the winged eyebrows and followed the curve of her cheekbone until it rested under her chin, then he forced her head up so that she had to face him.

'You're fighting me, Bridget. I can feel it in every nerve of your body. You haven't denied that there's a barrier between us. Have I committed some unforgivable sin? I can't associate you with pettiness, but if my smart-alec remarks when you first arrived still rankle, then I most sincerely apologise. Could you pardon me, whatever the reason, and let us be friends?'

'No. I don't want your friendship.' The answer burst from her without thought.

'Ah, now you're starting to be honest.' His brown eyes smiled down into her more-green-than-hazel ones. 'I thought all Christians had to love everyone, even their enemies.'

'I'm not perfect yet,' Bridget muttered fiercely. 'I'm just learning. Let me go! This is ridiculous.'

'It is, isn't it?' Gareth did not seem perturbed. 'But I'm determined to find the cause of your animosity, so we can stay here all night if you like. You see, I wouldn't bother, except that I have this thought haunting me that we've met before . . .'

'That's an old line,' she jeered, then added in a simpering lisp, 'Bet you thay that to all the girlth.'

He laughed. 'As a matter of fact, I don't. Only you, Bridget. Tell me, so you have this feeling that we've met before?'

'If we had met before, I'm sure I would *not* have forgotten it,' she said fiercely.

'You have a point there. I feel that if I'd met a girl like you anywhere in my life I'd be able to remember. Worse than that, I have this feeling that we were friends, that in some way we were close, that your company was dear to me. Sometimes the way you turn your head, the way you laugh, reinforces this feeling, yet it slips away again. You intrigue me.'

'Go and find someone else to intrigue you,' Bridget replied angrily.

'I can't now that I've kissed you. There was something between us, something hidden and deep. I may have met you before but, by hokey, I'll bet I never kissed you. That I would never forget.'

Bridget remained stubbornly silent.

'You're still fighting me, but you're not going to win. I am.' Gareth's eyes were dark and compelling, 'Your coming here hasn't been an accident, I'm positive of that. It's as if someone had given me an extremely valuable volume, exquisitely bound, in gold and purple, and told me that inside there would be the most exciting and fascinating story and when I went to open it, I found that it was locked and they'd forgotten to give me the key.'

'Who would expect a high country farmer to have such a vivid and far-fetched imagination? The story of my life is dull and boring and you'd be sadly disappointed if you ever heard it.'

'So you're not prepared to help me?' asked Gareth.

'I'm not.'

'Do you know that when you look at Jamie, your eyes are like summer seas, and golden sands, clear and warm, and when you talk to me they're green like a mysterious and lonely pool in the depths of the forest, shaded and cool. But no matter, I like a challenge, and I *will* know you, Bridget, hide what you will!'

His head bent towards her, and she waited with

her eyes closed for his kiss. Her blood pounded and her very bones seemed to melt, and she knew that if he kissed her she would fight no more. She was beaten. Then she felt his hands release her and, when she opened her eyes, he had left the room. She leaned back against the sink bench for support, shaken to the very depths of her soul. She had not expected Gareth to confront her and try to bring everything out in the open, but she should have done so. It was never his way to avoid an issue, even if it was unpleasant. Well, she had survived, but only just . . . then she started to giggle almost hysterically. She was sure he was the first man who nearly got his face slapped for *not* kissing a girl! There she had been—eyes closed, lips all waiting and ready, and he had just walked away and left her, not knowing that victory had been within his grasp.

She walked through to check the children and saw her flushed and burning cheeks in the mirror, her eyes brilliant and shining. Oh, yes, she could be honest with herself if not with Gareth. She had fallen in love with him again, completely and devastatingly in love, and it was worse, much worse, than the time before . . . and in a strange way, better, much better. She would let it develop and grow because she knew no way of stopping it. She loved him, and his ways were dear, so very dear to her, but she would never let him see that love. There were only another four weeks to go, and if she could only carry on as she had been going, at least she would not have so much forgetting to do.

She sat by the fire, starry-eyed, reliving the moment in the moonlight, adding it to the store of precious memories, that were hers and hers alone. Falling in love again was something she could not help and going over old remembrances of the friendship they had once shared could not hurt her. Only dreaming dreams of the future was the ultimate stupidity, and she would refrain from that. There would be no 'what-might-have-beens' to eradicate when she left here. Once she had dreamed and planned of being part of him and his life, of sharing whatever joys and hardships that came to him, of bearing his children, of being his chosen one, his helpmate, but those dreams had disintegrated in the harsh glare of reality, when she learned that he planned to marry that other girl.

The fact that he was still single did not mean she wasn't there somewhere in the background. Bridget had given up all thought of marriage and children, and to bring those dreams back to life, and then lose them again, would be unendurable.

He was just responding to the challenge of finding out something about her which she would not tell him. There was nothing more than that and she was not going to read more into his behaviour than that. He was also a little piqued that she preferred Jamie's company. It was probably the first time in his life he hadn't been first choice in anyone's preference listings. It would do him good.

Jamie was nice. He was like her in a way. He had made his choice to remain single ... something about, 'he travels fastest who travels alone'. He had said it with a hint of hardness which made her know immediately that some painful experience had moulded his choice. They had not discussed it, but instinctively Bridget knew he would make no demands on her, that like her, he only wanted a casual friendship. The knowledge pleased her. To be liked and to have her company appreciated at this time was like having a soothing balm covering an unhealed wound.

Kathy and Doug came in together, laughing and relaxed. 'Jamie is putting his car away. He said he wouldn't bother with coffee. Have the children been good, Bridget? Oh, you don't know how good it was to enjoy myself without them! I love them dearly, but just to have time to be by myself without the responsibility of worrying about them was heavenly. I love you for thinking of it. You're a darling!'

Bridget was smiling. 'Feel free to take off any time I'm here. You look ten years younger, which probably makes you about fifteen. The kids have been good, but I have to admit I'm looking forward to my bed, so don't take offence if I don't stay for coffee, either. Did you enjoy yourself, too, Doug?'

'I certainly did. Kathy here is a real charmer and kidded me into dancing again . . . I haven't danced for years, but with a partner like her, it came easy.'

'I'm pleased. See you both in the morning.' Bridget slipped out the door, glad she had not shared her worry about Valinda with them. Why spoil their night? But in spite of her father's advice she knew she would get no sleep. How could she sleep with Valinda wandering around the city feeling unloved and unwanted? What mischief and trouble would she launch into to prove she needed nobody? With her heart heavy Bridget prepared for bed, and it was a long time before she slept.

The sun was well up when she woke and, shocked at herself for sleeping so late, she flung on her robe and ran to Valinda's room, but it was empty and the bed had not been slept in.

Slowly Bridget returned to her own room and dressed. She had been sure that Valinda would come home during the night. She walked to the window and felt the cool fresh wind on her face, and her spirits rose as she filled her soul with the beauty of the sunlit valley spread out before her—the jewelled beauty of the lake, the golden-brown of the tussock hills and the snow-capped giants, majestic, awesome, piercing the incredible blueness of the sky. She had been here such a short while, so why did she have such a sense of belonging? This valley had a timeless beauty. The first Curtis, who had claimed it as his promised land and named the river and the hills, would have felt the same awe and wonder as he had gazed at it as she did now, and a hundred years from now it would still thrill new eyes afresh. Man could use it or abuse it, sow his seed, feed his stock, nurture and care for it, and it would prosper him, or he could ignore it and neglect it, and fail financially, but basically he could not change or alter the wild and lonely sweep of the hills and plain or the shape and outline of the jagged amethyst peaks.

Deer would still roam these mountains and wild ducks, and geese would still follow the green and silver ribbon of the river when she was back in England; the pigeons and tuis would still feed on the berries and nectar of the garden trees and fill the morning air with their song when she was gone, and she was filled with an unquestioned longing to stay, never to leave, to grow old here as Miss Curtis had.

Resolutely she put the thought from her. She must not indulge in dreams. She stopped by the mirror, searching the planes and angles of her face, tracing thoughtfully the delicate outline of her chin and cheek, almost unconsciously following the pattern of Gareth's exploring finger last night. With deep gratitude she knew there was no way he could connect the pudding-faced, currant-eyed Bonnie with the elegant, fine-boned contours which were reflected back at her.

She ran down the stairs, confident of her ability to maintain her shield of mystery against any of Gareth's probing. So he enjoyed a challenge, did he? Well, she would give him one! The very thought of meeting him this morning sent her pulses racing, and her whole body was swept with a singing joy and a wild excitement that she could barely contain.

She loved Gareth Evans, and the knowledge was a sweet and wonderful secret that she would never share. She felt like a miser gloating over his gold in a locked vault, and Gareth could search in vain for the key to his memory bank, but she would give him no help, and he would fail. He would never know that he was so loved, that he was so very dear to her, that each smile he gave her was going to be stored up and treasured like fine gold, and that the kiss he gave her so carelessly last night was precious and rare beyond description.

If he knew that it was because of him Bridget had chosen never to marry, never to bear children, he would think her utterly ridiculous, and he wouldn't be far wrong. She did feel ridiculous when she thought about her decision, but that did not take away the certainty that, in the whole world, the only man she could want as a marriage partner and father for her children was Gareth Evans. She had known it four years ago, she had had that knowledge reinforced last night. There was a magnetism, a force within him that drew her with such power that no other man had any attraction for her. He was her other half, with him she would be complete, together they could have scaled the heights, or plumbed the depths, and have had a love that would have lasted for all eternity. Yet Gareth felt nothing for her—a casual friendship four years ago had been easily forgotten. And he would forget her just as swiftly this time. He was only interested because he felt a little annoyed that she had not responded to his offer of easy-come, easy-go friendship.

Well, this time she wouldn't get hurt, she would wear no battle scars for him. She would walk out of his life as lightly as she had walked in, and he would never know that he was all the world to her.

CHAPTER SIX

BRIDGET flung open the kitchen door and walked towards the table where the men were lingering over their coffee, enjoying the one day of the week that was without work. She laughed at their teasing remarks about being a sleepyhead and paused to cuddle Matthew in his high-chair, and drop a kiss on Kelly's eager, uplifted face, before taking her place by Kathy.

She caught the question in Gareth's brown eyes and shook her head. She would soon have to tell Miss Curtis and the others that Valinda had gone.

'There's a dragon on the lawn,' Kelly announced. 'Tan you see him, Bwidget? Mummy tan't see him. He's got fire toming out his nose, see?'

Bridget turned to search for the imaginary dragon, and her heart leapt for joy as she saw the Morris curve towards the car shed. Valinda was home! She half rose, then sat down again. How was she supposed to act? Should she pretend there was nothing wrong? If she was angry, Valinda might take off again, and if she was over-effusive, she could do just as much harm.

'You doan see my dragon too,' Kelly protested. 'Do you see him, Doug?'

Doug could not resist the appeal. 'Sure I can, Kelly. He's over there by the tree. Do you think he's friendly? Maybe you could have a ride on him. Come on, I've finished my breakfast, we'll go and put a saddle on him.'

Kelly gave him a suspicious look to check if he was serious or laughing at her, then, satisfied, ran to catch his hand and drag him with her.

Gareth laughed, 'That kid is special, Kathy. If she can wind a bloke like Doug round her little finger at three, you'll be picking up a lot of broken hearts later on!'

They all watched the big, fair man putting an imaginary saddle on a wooden box and lift the delighted Kelly on, then hand her the reins, and saw Valinda stop and speak with them before walking up the path.

Jamie pushed back his chair noisily. 'I'll go and saddle the horses, Bridget. Could you put us up a bit of lunch? It's a beaut day for it.'

Before he could leave the room, Valinda came in. 'Hi, everyone. Did you have a good night out? I did.'

Bridget's heart sank at the brittle flippancy in her voice. She felt totally inadequate. 'Would you like some breakfast, Valinda?' she asked casually. 'I'm late as well, so I'll make a fresh cup of tea for us both.'

'What do I get? Bread and water? Loss of privileges?' Valinda was ignoring everyone else in the room, and seemed to enjoy baiting Bridget. 'I expected to hear the police siren behind me all the time. Don't tell me you didn't ring them to report your car was stolen? You disappoint me. I took some money from your purse, too—didn't you check? It's easy to see you're not used to dealing with the criminal element. You're too easy to rip off.'

Bridget faced Valinda, the hurt showing in her eyes, because she could not conceal it. 'I didn't notify the police. You must have known I wouldn't do that.

I'm your friend. If you took money from me, you're welcome to it.' She bit her lip, fighting back the tears that threatened.

'Aren't you going to ask where I've been? Wouldn't you like all the gory details?'

Bridget shook her head. She could see beyond the boldness and brittleness in Valinda's eyes an appeal for help, but had no way of answering it. What did Valinda want from her? Why didn't Gareth speak? Or any of them? They were just leaving her to flounder around on her own. Of course she was supposed to be in charge of Valinda, but she needed help. Lord help me, she thought, if I say the wrong word now I'll lose her for all time. She'll storm out of here and it will all be over.

'I don't want to know where you've been, Valinda. I trust you. You're your own person, you'll do what you feel you must, but whatever you do I'll love you. I make no conditions. What you did last night, or last year, or what you will do tomorrow or next year won't change that fact.'

'Then why are you crying?' The voice was a little softer.

Bridget shrugged her shoulders. 'I don't know. Probably because I'm just so relieved to see you home.'

'Yes, you're as stupid as that.' Valinda's voice held a sob. 'Here's your keys. And I'm sorry I upset you. I'm sorry I took your car without permission. I spent the night with Jody's mother and father. They're like you—soft. They told me to come back here. They said that's what Jody would expect me to do. But if you'd come the heavy with me, I'd have cleared out for good. I didn't mean to be so hard on you, but I had to know.'

'Yes, you had to know,' Bridget agreed, feeling a flood of relief.

'Well, I'd better go and humble myself before Great-Aunt Grace,' shrugged Valinda.

'She doesn't know you've been away, so there's no need for you to tell her. Only Gareth and I knew.'

'Thanks, both of you,' Valinda said simply, and left the room.

Bridget sank into her chair, her legs too weak to support her, then glared at Gareth. 'You were a lot of help!' she snapped. 'You could have said something.'

'What? It was between you and Valinda—I told you that last night. You did well.' His brown eyes held such warmth that Bridget had to dive into her pocket to retrieve her handkerchief again.

Jamie walked around the table and gave her a reassuring hug. 'Magnificent! I thought you were going to miss there for a bit. That was one tough scene. If she wants to ride with us, tell her she's welcome. Maybe there's more to that kid than I thought. It took guts to come back.' He turned by the door. 'Half an hour, Bridget.'

Gareth followed him. 'I might come with you. I wouldn't mind taking a look at all the possibilities myself. Any objection?'

Jamie grinned, 'Good idea—we'll make a day of it.'

Thankfully Bridget took the strong, fresh cup of tea that Kathy had made. 'That was a nice gesture of Jamie's. I'm glad he's changed his mind about Valinda. She needs people to approve of her if she's going to make it.'

Kathy hefted Matthew from his high-chair and opened the door to let him stagger joyfully out to join Doug and Kelly. 'Yes, he's a nice guy, Jamie. Quiet, you know, but he's really come out of his shell since you came here. Someone told me once that he'd been wrapped up in a young girl who played him fast and loose for several years. She was just amusing herself with him, and when he found out he was pretty bitter. I hope he doesn't fall for Valinda, though, she could do the same thing to him.'

'Valinda's all right,' Bridget protested.

Kathy laughed, 'You've got a mother-hen complex, but your chick is a bit of a tiger! Still, Jamie's older now, and a lot more cautious. He'll be harder to catch this time, a bit like Gareth.'

'Why? Did Gareth get his fingers burned, too?' Bridget hoped she didn't sound too interested.

Kathy poured herself a cup of tea. 'Frankly, I don't know what happened to Gareth. He was engaged for a couple of years. She was a real smasher, but not really his style. They looked superb together, but there was no spark, almost as if they got engaged because they'd always gone around together and it was expected that they'd eventually marry. I was glad when it fizzled out. I'm a real Gareth fan, and I'd have hated to see him tied to her for life, she seemed so shallow, no substance, no brains.'

It was crazy of Bridget to be so absurdly pleased that Kathy had not liked his fiancée. 'So nobody got hurt?'

'Not really. I always got the impression that he knew he'd made a mistake and was too much a gentleman to break it off, and too canny to let it get as far as the altar. He just stalled for time and waited for her to get interested somewhere else.'

'A real Sir Galahad,' Bridget said sarcastically.

'We all make mistakes. I'm glad his wasn't a life

sentence. He'll marry some day, he's not bachelor material, and the girl that gets him will be exceptionally lucky. I reckon he's never been in love, but some day he's going to fall like a pack of cards—and boy, he'll be hard to resist! I bet he sweeps her off with such speed he'd make Young Lochinvar look a real slowpoke.'

Bridget laughed, 'What a fate! I'm glad I'm not a candidate. I'll hop up and see if Valinda wants to come with us, and then make the lunches.'

She took the stairs lightly, and knocked on Valinda's door. Valinda was lying stretched out on the bed, 'What's up?' she queried.

'I wondered if you'd like to go with us up to Hell's Gate. Jamie said to ask you.'

'Did you twist his arm?'

'No.'

'Then why did he invite me? He didn't want me last night.' Valinda's tone was belligerent.

'He just said, if she wants to go with us, tell her she's welcome. Then he said something about it must have taken guts to come home. Gareth is going too, and I have to pack lunch. If you want to come, get off that bed and come and help me.'

Valinda bounced off the bed as if jet-propelled. 'I'll get on my riding gear. You start, I'll be down in a minute.' She whirled across the room, then spun on her foot and raced over to give Bridget a hug. 'Jody sure can pick people!'

Bridget went downstairs feeling warmed by Valinda's hug, but wondering if she deserved it. It had been Jamie's generosity that had brought Valinda's swift change of mood. Had Bridget's own moods been so merciful when she was seventeen— up one moment and down the next? No, hers had all been downers until she met Gareth, and she hadn't changed at all. He was coming with them, and she was so happy she was delirious.

They were ready when Jamie whistled for them, and Bridget was pleased to see Valinda walk directly up to Jamie and thank him for allowing her to travel with them. She sighed. Valinda was so like the little girl who had a little curl right in the middle of her forehead . . . when she was good she was very, very good and when she was bad she was horrid!

The horses were fresh and the strong wind blowing seemed to excite them—they tossed their heads and pranced with eagerness to be away.

Four abreast, they cantered across the wide tussock-covered plain towards the river, and Bridget felt that for ever she would hold inside her the matchless beauty of the morning, and the joy of riding beside Gareth, and the thankfulness in her whole being that Valinda was here with them. Her amethyst hills to the east had lost more snow, but, deep and purple-shadowed, they were just as grand. Jamie winked at her, and she felt her cup was overflowing. Did it really matter that she was to be here such a short while? Her spirit had found a new release and her heart a new song of jubilation. She would live every moment to the full, even the rhythmic beat of the horses' hooves on the hard ground had a magic sound.

At the river she hesitated when Jamie and Valinda plunged in with a shower of water spraying out from their horses.

'Let Nadia have her head. She's a sound water horse, and will pick her own path. Just keep your feet clear of the water.'

Gareth had waited for her and, keeping his big

horse downstream of her, gave her the confidence to
nudge Nadia into action. The river ran wide and
swift and Bridget had turned to smile her thanks at
his thoughtfulness, when the look in his steadfast gaze
made her heart turn somersaults, and she hastily
looked down. The rushing water made her slightly
giddy, but it was better than trying to read Gareth's
expression.

Once out of the water, the horses soon had to walk
single file up a narrow track that rose steeply above
the river, and Bridget's heart was in her mouth until
they reached the plateau. From there she turned to
look back at the homestead and was surprised to see
how small and distant it had become. The country
took on a more rugged appearance and they rode
through bush and scrub which threatened to dislodge
her. It seemed to her they had been hours in the
saddle, following a clear bubbling stream up a valley
that grew more and more narrow.

Finding herself beside Valinda, she asked, 'Do you
have any idea where we're heading? Jamie said
something about wild cattle, but I haven't seen a
thing.'

Valinda laughed. 'You won't either, unless you
know what you're looking for—they're much too
smart. About ten years ago old Jim decided to buy
some Aberdeen Angus cattle for the station. He
should have known better, because they're murder
to muster, and once he put them out they went wild.
They made their way across the river and through a
gorge we call Hell's Gate because it's so tough to get
stock through. Up there is a fantastic hanging valley,
and that's where they stayed. Plenty of people have
had a go at getting them out, but they're really
cunning. Jamie was telling me that they're the reason

he came to work here, he wants a chance at bringing them back. Gareth could well use the money on the station, so he's pretty keen too. Neither of them have been up here before, but they've talked to others who've tried, and looked at maps. They both think it's possible, but today they're just looking. Is your saddle getting hard?'

Bridget grimaced, 'I wish I'd brought a cushion!'

'It's not far now. I have to admit I'm tired too, but the view is tremendous across the mountains. You can see for miles.'

'Like being on top of the world,' Bridget agreed, before the track narrowed again and Nadia eased back to follow Valinda's horse over a natural rock ledge above the stream and between steep-sided cliffs.

They emerged from the dark gorge to overlook a fantastic sunlit valley, ringed by bush and dotted with cattle grazing, unaware of their presence. Breathless, Bridget watched three deer standing watching, with pricked ears and uplifted heads, a few hundred yards away, then they bounded off with white tails flashing. Their action alerted the cattle and within seconds they were disappearing towards the other end of the valley.

'You've lost them,' Bridget said sadly.

Gareth dismounted. 'No. They can't get out of here except the way we came in, or over that low saddle to our right. We'll have lunch, then you girls rest here while Jamie and I have a scout around.'

'It'll have to be in the saddle,' said Jamie. 'No wonder they lost them here at the Gate, there's no way you could crowd wild cattle in there. The entrance is too abrupt, they'd beat you every time. I'll boil the billy.'

As the girls unpacked the lunch, Valinda asked, 'When are you going to try and muster them out, Gareth? Can Bridget and I be part of it? You'd have to camp here the night and start at daybreak, wouldn't you? That would be fun.'

'Fun and hard work. Yes, you'll still be here. The Government lease expires at the end of the month, anything left here then will be shot and taken out, so I haven't got long. Fancy sleeping out under the stars, Bridget?' His brown eyes were bright and teasing.

Jamie handed Bridget her mug of tea. 'Of course Bridget will come. I couldn't manage without her.'

'You have your answer, Gareth.' Her eyes were very, very green.

'This is how land should look, open and unfenced.' Jamie leaned on his elbow looking up the valley. 'I know just how the cattlemen in Texas must have felt when the sheep came and the herders started stringing up bits of wire. I was born in the wrong age, but nobody is going to fence me in. Bridget's like me—a free spirit. We're going to roam the world together.'

'Is that how you see her?' Gareth asked.

'Of course. No marriage, mortgage, nappies, and kids, eh, Bridget?'

'That's right, Jamie,' Bridget agreed, smiling at him.

'Funny you should say that.' Gareth took another sandwich. 'I watch you with Kathy's kids and see you as a perfect wife and mother, rushing to the door to greet her husband with a loving kiss.'

Bridget felt her cheeks grow hot and knew he was referring to the previous night, and avoided his gaze.

Valinda laughed, 'If you'd seen her when she

came to our school . . . no, it's okay, Bridget, I won't tell, but you certainly have changed. Tell me, Jamie, haven't you ever thought of getting married?'

'Yes. I was once madly in love, and thought I'd die if the girl didn't say she'd marry me. Shows how crazy you can be! She did me a big favour. You got closer to losing your freedom than I did, Gareth. You were engaged, weren't you? Aren't you glad you escaped the noose?'

'Yes, I am, but only because I chose the wrong girl.' He caught Bridget's quick glance and held her eyes. 'I'm glad I waited. During the war, soldiers said you couldn't be killed by a bomb or a bullet unless it had your name on it. Well, I'm waiting till I meet the girl who has my name written on her, and when I do find her I won't let her get away.'

Bridget's hand jerked and sent hot tea cascading down her arm. 'Damn!' She jumped up and ran over to the stream and held it in the ice-cold water, wishing she could plunge her burning face in as well. Gareth was flirting with her. How dared he? She was furious. He was just trying to make her drop her defences. If the others twigged what he was up to they'd be amused, and her life would become impossible. She wished she was a thousand miles away.

'Show me your arm. Not too much damage, I hope?' Gareth spoke just behind her.

She shot to her feet and held her hand behind her back childishly. 'None at all.' She would not look at him.

'Good. I'd hate you to get hurt.'

She could hear the laughter in his voice, and side-stepped him swiftly, muttering, 'There's no danger that I will.'

She could hear him chuckle and knew, as he did,

that neither of them had been referring to her sore arm.

It was a real relief to watch the men mount up and ride down the valley, and help Valinda pack up, then stretch out on the tussock grass and close her eyes. She didn't want to talk to anyone. She was angry at Gareth, but even more angry at herself. If she had treated him in a normal manner, his curiosity would not have been aroused. Then to top that off she had made it a personal challenge. What an idiot she had been! The whole situation was of her own making, and instead of crowing over her smartness in hiding her identity, she had highlighted the very point where she was most vulnerable.

'Gareth is a real romantic, isn't he?' commented Valinda. 'I got all goose-bumpy when he talked about the girl he was going to marry.'

'Uhuh.' Bridget tried to feign sleep.

Valinda was not so easily put off. 'He was watching you when he was speaking. I think he rather fancies you.'

'Rubbish! They were just talking nonsense, the pair of them.'

'Oh, I don't know. Do you think, then, that Jamie wants to get married?'

'Is it important to you?' asked Bridget.

Valinda rolled over, and made herself more comfortable on the tussocks, 'Not really. Actually I think he's more my style than Gareth. I don't believe in marriage myself. I mean, watching Mother and Dad hasn't exactly been any advertisement for it. By the way, did you ring Dad last night?'

'No.'

'Pity. He would have loved another chance to bemoan my shocking behaviour. You did him no favour. He expects the worst, why deny him the simple pleasures of life?'

'You sound very bitter, Valinda,' said Bridget. 'What did he do to you to make you so hard? You told me you're not his child. Did he make it obvious to you when you were little? Did he treat you differently from the rest of the children?'

Valinda was silent for so long Bridget thought she was not going to answer her. Perhaps the subject was better left alone.

'It's strange you should ask that,' she said at last. 'I was well behind the other kids and I seemed to be his favourite. The others were always going on about the fact that he spoiled me. I really thought he loved me.'

Bridget heard the pain in her voice. 'I've only spoken to him on the phone a couple of times and I believe he loves you. What made you think he didn't?'

'Well, he couldn't, could he? When I heard him and Mother yelling at each other that night, I knew. Nobody except a saint could love a cuckoo in the nest. I mean, I was a daily reminder to both of them. So I switched off.'

'Poor man!' said Bridget.

'Poor nothing! He'd always known. I was the sucker!' Valinda shouted. 'Your sympathy is always for the wrong side. You were sorry for Old Adam. I could see that made sense because she was inadequate, but my father isn't inadequate in any sense. Wait till you meet him!'

'He's inadequate in this situation. He can't reach you. That must really hurt him. Think about him for a moment. All your life he's given you his best, and you must have been a darling kid, and I can tell

by the things you've said that you had a special relationship with him, a real bonding. Then one night
you hear a quarrel and cut him completely out of
your life. Did you tell him why? Give any reason?'

'You're joking!' jeered Valinda.

'Well, he wouldn't have a clue,' Bridget pointed
out. 'Did he deserve that? Couldn't you have been
honest and talked it over with him?'

'I could not!' Valinda's voice was savage.

'Well, I think you should give it serious thought. I
think he did something very fine . . . if what you say
is true . . . he put everything away from him, and
never let it affect his attitude towards you, he
accepted you as his own from the moment you were
born and loved you. Have you found him lacking in
integrity or honesty in any other part of his life?'

'No.' The tone was muffled.

'Then maybe you should accept his love as real
and genuine. If you'd been an adopted child, and
neither one of them your true physical parents,
would you have resented them when you found out,
or would you have thought of all the love and care
they'd lavished on you more than recompense for
not telling you the whole truth earlier? Adoptive
parents love the child as their own, and I think your
father loved you as his very own child. Look, people
say dreadful things to each other when they're fighting, things that aim to hurt and destroy, and quite
often they're not true at all. But whether what you
heard was true or false, I think you should talk it
out with him.'

'I just might.' Valinda made it sound like a threat.
I'll give it thought.'

'Great! Now I'm going to grab some sleep or I'll
never make it home.'

There was a short silence, then Valinda spoke again. 'You're a strange one, Bridget. Can you see good in everyone?'

'I try.'

'I bet you'd even try and find something worthwhile in my mother. But you'd have to look pretty deep.'

'Have you ever tried looking deep?' Bridget asked.

'Not worth the effort. She's like a bluefly buzzing upstream backwards, never still for a moment. Golf, bridge, drama, committees, parties, antique furniture, good causes, her life is crammed full of useless activity. Dad was the only real thing in my life, then Jody. Mother did all the right things, said all the right things, but looking back, I can't remember her cuddling me, or doing one loving thing.'

'I don't know her,' said Bridget. 'But you've admitted you've never tried to know her. You can't understand anyone, to quote an old saying, until you've walked a mile in their shoes.'

'They wouldn't fit,' Valinda said flippantly. 'Go on, find some reason for me to be sorry for her. You're good at that.'

Bridget sighed. How she wished she was older, more experienced, had some training, because the questions Valinda was demanding answers for were outside her range. She realised that, in spite of her jeering tone, the girl was wanting to find something good in her mother, something to love.

'Got you stumped!' Valinda jeered.

'No, not really. I just wish I knew your parents better. Anything I say will be pure conjecture. But if I were to try and put myself in her place, from what you've told me, the first thing that would come to my mind would be the load of guilt she must have carried all these years. Perhaps your father did forgive her, but never trusted her again. That would be hard to take, if she was genuinely sorry for her mistake and tried to make it up to him, and he never gave her a chance. I'm not blaming him, I'm just saying that maybe she gave up trying and filled her life with other things. Maybe he did forgive her fully, and she couldn't forgive herself.'

Bridget glanced at Valinda, who was pulling pieces of tussock grass out and arranging them into an elaborate pattern, but there was no doubt she was listening intently.

'This would have been happening when you were too small to be aware of it. Say they had a really happy marriage, that your mother really loved your father, but when the children started school, and your father was very involved in building up his law practice and political career, she may have felt unwanted, unnecessary, bored . . . who knows? In a weak moment she became susceptible to an attractive man who flattered her, wanted her, and she may not even have cared for him very much, just wanted the attention your father wasn't giving her. It happens every day, Valinda. Can you imagine how she'd feel? In one foolish act she destroyed the fabric of a whole family. You say they only stayed together because of the material advantages, family name, etc., but what if they stayed together because they loved each other? How much worse the pain would be if they couldn't rebuild that trust and love? Could you feel sorry for her, if the circumstances were something like that?'

Valinda sprang to her feet and savagely kicked away the pattern she had been constructing. 'I'm going for a walk. I think you'd find excuses for the devil himself!'

'That I would not!' Bridget shouted after Valinda's retreating figure, then lay back in the warm sunlight, feeling completely exhausted. How did professionals manage not to get involved with the people they were trying to help? She was involved up to her eyebrows because she loved Valinda and wanted to help her through this bad patch more than she had ever wanted anything ... well, anything except Gareth. She wanted to ring her father and scream at him to tell her what to say, or come out here himself, yet she knew what his answer would be—'Love her. Love conquers fear, love heals.'

She woke to the sounds of horses' hooves thundering across the valley towards her and sat up just before the men arrived. The sun had lowered in the west and the horses and riders were dark silhouettes against the apricot sky and the silver-trimmed clouds. The wild beauty of the lonely valley, the music of the mountain stream, and the horsemen riding made Bridget feel she was part of some dream sequence, but as a spectator, not a participant. She shivered. She wanted to be more than a spectator watching life from a distance, yet the years of conditioning herself, as a fat and awkward child, to expect rejection and to armour herself against it, had made that armour so strong that it had almost become a prison. Gareth had been the first person, except her parents, to reach past that carefully erected wall, and all her defences had crumbled and dissolved in the warmth of his love. Then he had forgotten her and the walls had been rebuilt, stronger this time, and she would be a fool to risk that pain again, yet she was losing the battle and she knew it. The sweet surge of exhilaration and joy which swept through her like a torrent each time he spoke to her or smiled that endearing grin made her long to throw caution to the winds and trust him again. Her very bones ached with the irresistible longing to respond, to seek again that special intimacy with him, to be in his favour.

'Sorry to be so late, but we decided to see how difficult it would be to gather them up.' Gareth smiled down at Bridget. 'We mustered out a couple of small side valleys and they moved well. Have you been bored?'

'Not at all. I had a sleep. I'd better get my horse. Or do you want something more to eat?'

Jamie dismounted. 'We'd better get on our way to get out of the wilderness before dark. You've got apples there?'

Bridget handed them an apple each and turned to find Valinda bringing the horses up. 'Apple?' she offered.

'Peace-offering?' Valinda asked.

'Have you two been fighting?' Jamie gave her a sharp look.

'Bridget wasn't. I was,' Valinda told him with a grin. 'Bridget loves everybody, it must be an awful handicap.' She traded Nadia's reins for an apple. 'Sorry for yelling at you, Bridget. When I cooled down I knew you were right. It's better to talk things out. When Dad gets back I'll front up.'

'I'm glad,' smiled Bridget.

Valinda's grin was warm and friendly. 'I thought you just might be. I used to believe that if I rattled the skeletons in the cupboard, it would only make things worse, but now I know they couldn't be worse, so I'll try for a bit of your devasting honesty—it might clear the air. You'll stick around to pick up the pieces?'

'I'll be there if you need me,' Bridget assured her, before swinging into her saddle.

The trip home seemed so much shorter to Bridget. Maybe because the horses were more eager, or maybe because each time the track widened enough for two horses, she found herself riding beside Gareth.

'Why did you come here, Gareth? Jamie said he works here because most of the stations are becoming too mechanised and he loves horses.' Bridget was still puzzled as to why he wasn't in the farming complex up north.

'Fate, of course. Just so I could meet you.' Gareth's smile was wicked.

'Rubbish!' Bridget felt her cheeks burn. 'Why can't you be serious with me?'

'Oh, but I'm deadly serious about you, young Bridget.'

Bridget felt her blush must rival the crimson rays of the setting sun, and she dug her heels in to urge Nadia to move past Gareth, but he reached out a hand and caught the bridle, and she was furiously helpless. Worse, he was riding so close—knee to knee—that she felt he would be able to read her real emotions like an open book.

He released the bridle and straightened up. 'Don't try to ride away from me, Bridget—I won't let you. From what Valinda was saying you've been giving her a lecture on being open and honest in her dealings with her father. Very commendable, but you don't follow your own advice. You're not honest with me.'

'The circumstances are different,' Bridget protested, knowing he was speaking the truth. 'She's trying to establish a relationship that will endure.'

'So am I.'

'Well, I'm not!' Bridget's green eyes were clear and bright.

Gareth roared with laughing. 'Now there's the devastating honesty Valinda was talking about! Serve me right. You asked what brought me to Paradise Peaks? A few years back we had one of those family celebrations, and there was a gathering of the clan, so to speak, and an aunt of mine traced out a history of the family from the time my mother's people first arrived here. Apparently there were a couple of brothers and one went to the North Island and one to the South. Well, travel was difficult in those days and I suppose letters were few, but as the generations developed the two families lost all contact. However, there was one letter kept, in which the brother who took up land here at Paradise Peaks described it to his brother up North. I read it and it caught my imagination, so when I came South four years ago, I searched this place out and was really impressed with it.'

'So you're related to Miss Curtis and Valinda?'

'No, I'd hardly claim that, four or five generations come in between now, so there's no real blood tie. I've never mentioned it to them and would prefer it if you didn't. It would look as if I was trying to get my feet under their table when I have no right to it. Actually, when I first saw the place, I just felt sorry that it hadn't worked out like the first chap expected. That was over four years ago and I was down here in the South getting a bit of experience before going into partnership with my father and brother up North.'

'What happened?' Bridget cursed her curiosity, but she wanted to know. She would regret later that she had encouraged him to share with her, she should be indifferent, but she wasn't.

'Plans have a way of coming unstuck,' he shrugged. 'I went home, of course, but playing third fiddle there held no appeal. It was too commercial; everything planned on computers, organised down to the last blade of grass. I felt like having a go on my own, so I came back South, and this place came back in my mind. It wouldn't go away, and I kept seeing what it would look like if someone started with modern ideas and brought it in to full production. The place has fantastic potential.'

'You want to buy it?' Bridget's eyes were round with surprise.

'That's the general idea. I went to the land agents and found that no one in the family was keen on it. So when Miss Curtis dies it will go on the market. I looked at many other places, but none had the same attraction. Then the other bit was the family connection—I know it's fairly vague and tenuous after a hundred years, but I thought it a shame that nobody cared about it at all. I felt like putting flesh on the dreams the first Curtis had when he took this place up here, in the eighties. Sounds crazy now I've put it into words.'

'It doesn't. I think it's a wonderful idea.' Her eyes were shining.

'Well, the agents knew I had an interest in the place, and they got in touch with me when Jim had his stroke a few months back, and asked me to come here as manager. It suited me fine.'

'I think you should tell Miss Curtis your plans,' said Bridget. 'She'd be pleased.'

'She might not be. She may think of me as a vulture waiting for her to die. I know it's not like that, and I would hate to upset her. The solicitor and the agent agree with me. She hasn't had an easy life here. She had two brothers as well as a sister, who was Valinda's grandmother. Both brothers were killed, one in an accident here on the farm in the thirties, and the other one in the war. Up till then the place was going ahead in fine style, but when the second son was killed her father lost heart, and as he got older, he left most of the running of it to managers. When he died, Angel did the same, and as you can see it's almost reverted to the original state. I hope I can bring it back. It will be a challenge, but as I told you the other night, I enjoy a challenge.'

Bridget was glad they had reached the narrow track leading to the river as that meant she did not have to reply to Gareth's last remark. Once across the river and out on the tussock plain, the wind was too strong for conversation, and she was pleased about that too. How quickly had she identified herself with his plans. Why, already she was viewing the darkening valley as his! He had trusted her enough to share his plans with her and in spite of herself she felt privileged. She was stupid. More than likely Kathy and Jamie knew, too. But she felt special and she couldn't deny it.

By the time they had stripped the saddles and bridles and loosed the horses, Bridget, being the slowest, was last out of the stable and found Gareth leaning on the gate waiting to escort her to the house.

'You needn't have waited,' she said rather aggressively.

'My pleasure, my very great pleasure.' Again his voice held amusement.

Bridget bit her lip, and walked warily wide of him. In her hurry to reach the safety of the lighted house she didn't look where she was placing her feet and suddenly measured her length on the ground.

Gareth helped her to her feet. 'Not hurt? Good. If you'd taken my arm, I could have saved you the indignity of adding to the urban sprawl. Remember you're still a bit of a townie and you haven't got night eyes for the country yet.'

Bridget laughed. 'I suppose it did look funny. Urban sprawl—that describes it!'

He kept hold of her arm and at the garden gate he stopped her. 'You know, Bridget, that's the very first time you've laughed with me. I like the sound. We're moving ahead, aren't we?'

She tried to pull away, but he held her quite firmly without hurting her and her heart thudded in her throat. He couldn't mean he was going to kiss her right here in the light from the kitchen window? Her legs felt weak and rubbery.

'You know when Jamie and I were talking at lunch time, I said I was waiting to meet a girl who had my name written on her?' said Gareth softly. 'Well, I think I've found her.'

Bridget panicked and twisted her arm free. 'Congratulations. I think you're pretty slow. I knew the moment I saw you together that you and Kathy were made for each other.'

She ran up the path, and looked back over her shoulder as she reached the door. He was still standing there in the moonlight by the gate, laughing at her. She could kill him!

She tried to steady her breathing, then stepped

into the kitchen. The aroma of the meal Kathy was serving was mouthwatering and she was ravenous after her day outdoors, but she'd rather die than face Gareth again tonight.

She crossed quickly to Kathy, thankful that Kelly was preoccupied with a story Doug was reading her. 'Don't serve anything for me, Kathy. I'm too tired to eat. I'm going straight to bed.'

Before Kathy could answer, Bridget disappeared through the door, and taking the stairs two at a time, ran for her room and slammed the door behind her. Then she felt safe, but she knew it was a temporary sanctuary. She had bitten off more than she could chew. She had ignored Gareth, rejected his offer of friendship, then somehow he had come to realise there was more behind it than just natural incompatibility, and when he had tried to find out she had made a mystery out of it, taunted him and laughed at him.

She could not blame him, only her stupid, stupid self. He had been quietly summing her up for the first two weeks and now he had found the weakest point in her armour. It wasn't fair, it just wasn't fair! He had found that when he flirted with her she just crumpled like a car fender in a head-on collision. She had no defence, only flight, and there was a limit to the places she could avoid him. She had to work all day with him, and share meals with him, and he wasn't going to let up on her. He was having too much fun teasing her.

Still seething, she stripped off her clothes and headed for the shower. Gareth had won hands down. Here she was sulking in her room, starving to death, and because of her sleep this afternoon, not at all tired. Well, she had to fill in the evening. She would wash her hair and write letters and try to work out some way of coping with his new approach.

She poured on the shampoo and lathered her hair and massaged her scalp until it hurt. Pity she couldn't wash Gareth out of her system the same way. She rinsed off her hair and repeated the shampoo process and again rinsed it, then wound a towel turban-style around her head and put on her robe.

An hour later, with her hair drying and free of tangles, she was again pacing her room like an angry tiger. She was still furious with herself and mad at Gareth and still hungry. She had never felt so helpless. She couldn't pack her bags and leave . . . there was Valinda. No, tomorrow morning she would have to go right back into the same situation, and she had to find some way of coping. Huh! She remembered her mother trying to help her handle the cruel teasing of the children when she was at primary school. She had been the obvious target, shy, plain, and fat, hopeless at games, and her mother's advice was to just ignore the ugly names they had called her.

'When they see you don't react, they'll lose interest'. It hadn't been much help then, because she had wanted so much to be friends and to play with them, but she learned to withdraw into herself and pretend the names like Fatso, and Dumpling and Slob, didn't hurt her. She learned not to cry, to bury herself in books, but it had not been easy.

Now even the advice was impossible. She could not help reacting. She loved Gareth Evans with her whole heart, and had loved him for four years. She was about as firm as a jelly or a marshmallow when it came to resisting his appeal. He had an unfair advantage. Sure, he didn't know it, but he was soon going to find out.

What if she told him the truth? What if she confessed that she was the Bonnie he'd been friends with years ago? He would want to know why she had not said so straight away, and an explanation was impossible. Imagine telling him that she had fallen in love with him, and was scared of doing it again. She would sound so stupid . . . she was stupid. He would be so embarrassed, then pity her for the fool she was. She would *not* suffer his pity.

There had to be a way out. She walked to the window and thrust her burning face out into the cool night air. The moonlight flooded the valley with an almost unearthly beauty, and the stars shone like sparkling diamonds.

She did not know how long she leaned on the windowsill filling her mind with the exquisite beauty of the star-studded sky and the silvered tussock plain and high mountain peaks, or when peace quietened her angry spirit, but it did. She took her pad and pen and decided to write the whole sorry story to her father. He might not be able to help her, but at least he'd offer her sympathy.

There was a knock at the door and she stiffened.

'Valinda here, Bridget. Are you still awake?' The door opened and Valinda came in, carrying a tray with a pot of tea and the thickest, juiciest, most delicious roast beef sandwiches Bridget had ever seen.

'You've saved my life, Valinda!' she smiled. 'I was about to put the mattress between two pillows and eat it.'

Valinda laughed, 'Don't thank me. It's Gareth's idea. He made the sandwiches—real haymakers.'

For a moment Bridget considered refusing them, but her hunger got the better of her.

'You can thank him from me,' she said.

'You'll have to do it yourself tomorrow morning. I'm off to bed. I've had it. Anyway, there's some sort of trouble between Gareth and Aunt Grace. After he'd made these he had to report to the library ... a command performance. I don't envy him— Aunt Grace is in a rare temper, and when she's like that she's immovable.'

'What's it about?' asked Bridget.

'Something about a car she ordered, and Gareth says she can't have it. Want to bet she'll win?'

'I'd put my money on Gareth.'

Valinda gave her an impish grin. 'You're on! If Aunt Grace can triumph over my father in battle she'll make mincemeat out of Gareth. The bet is ten dollars. Goodnight.'

When Bridget had eaten the last crumb of bread and drunk her third cup of tea, she felt quite benevolent and utterly replete. As she snuggled down under the covers she thought it was mean and despicable of Gareth to undermine her resentment by appealing to her most basic need. But she was smiling as she fell asleep.

CHAPTER SEVEN

KATHY turned from the stove as Bridget came into the kitchen. 'Hi, feeling better?'

'Terrific! Isn't it a wonderful morning? Thinking back, I can't remember it raining since I've been here. It's great weather.'

'Don't let Gareth hear you say that,' warned Kathy. 'He's getting a bit anxious for some rain. On the T.V. last night they were predicting a drought this year and it's not summer yet. In fact, if I were you, I wouldn't say too much to Gareth at all this morning. He's in a rare bad mood.'

'There goes my ten dollars,' Bridget said ruefully. Seeing Kathy's surprised look, she explained, 'Valinda told me that Gareth and Miss Curtis were having an argument about buying a car, and she bet me that he'd lose.'

Matthew was grizzling and trying to climb up Kathy's leg, so Bridget bent down and hoisted him on to her hips so he could see what was going on. 'Where's everyone?' she asked.

'Eaten and gone,' Kathy replied with a grim look. 'Gareth said you were to go straight out to him at the yards as soon as you came down.'

'Without my breakfast?' Bridget protested. 'I'm not late, they're early.'

'I wouldn't mention that either. Oh, I suppose I'd better tell you, although I don't know officially. Gareth had a colossal row with Miss Curtis last night and she fired him.'

Bridget stared at her in shock, 'Oh, no! How terrible!'

'Yes, it's bad. You'd better get straight out there.'

Kelly came flying out of her room. 'Tan I do with you, Bridget? I want to see the tows aden.'

Kathy spoke sharply, 'No, you can't, Kelly. You'll see the cows again another time. Put him down, Bridget. I can see this is going to be one of those days when I wish I'd stayed in bed!'

Bridget hurriedly left the room, with the sound of two children roaring in unison. Poor Kathy, and poor Gareth. What was going to happen? She tried to imagine Paradise Peaks with him gone, and suddenly the sunlight did not seem so bright.

She saw him striding from the yards towards the car-shed and changed her direction.

'Good—come with me' he invited. 'I want to see if you can drive Miss Curtis's big car. She's going through to Christchurch to see her lawyer and she won't allow me to drive her.. Here's the keys, hop in and I'll give you a test drive.'

If he wasn't going to tell her of the trouble Bridget certainly wasn't going to ask. She slid in behind the wheel. 'I can't see,' she said.

'Get out and I'll find the seat adjustment. There, that ought to do it. Do you think you can handle it? I hate to ask you really, but I've no option. She's set on going, and she's going to need someone sympathetic and sensitive to help her through.'

Bridget got in again and Gareth strode around and sat in the passenger seat. 'It's automatic. Have you ever driven one before?'

'Yes. I can drive Andrew's car.' She watched carefully as he explained the panel, then switched on and reversed out into the sunshine.

'Drive out to the main road and back. I want to be sure.'

Throughout the whole drive Gareth never spoke and Bridget concentrated on getting the feel of the car. When she had parked at the front door. she switched off and waited for him to speak.

Suddenly the frown cleared from his troubled face and he smiled. 'I knew I could count on you, Bridget. You're a wee beaùt.' He leaned over and gave her a hug, then got out of the car and came around to open her door.

'Listen carefully. I don't know what's going to happen when you get to Christchurch. You'll have to play it by ear. Miss Curtis and I had a bit of a set-to last night and she told me to leave. Legally she can't fire me, but it will depend how the lawyers explain it to her whether I'll be able to go on working here. She's a very stubborn and spirited old duck and I won't upset her if I can help it. If they can calm her down and get her to accept that it's in her best interests to keep me, we'll be right. If not . . .' His voice tailed off and his eyes swept the valley. 'We'll face that when it happens. All I want of you is to be with her, be kind to her, protect her if you can. She's not very strong physically, and a shock like this could be very hard on her.'

'Hard on you, too,' Bridget offered sympathetically. 'I'm sorry it happened. I'll do my best.'

Gareth's eyes met hers, 'I know you will. I trust you. It'll work out, you'll see.' He stretched out a hand and gave her head a pat and the next minute was striding towards the stables.

Tears blurred Bridget's vision. If only he wasn't so *easy* to love. He could be losing the place he had his heart set on, and all he could think of was how to protect and shelter Miss Curtis. And that quick hug had been so reminiscent of the times when she was his trusted friend and companion. It was a tricky situation, but she would do her best to soothe Miss Curtis, if she had the chance.

She went back to the kitchen to find Valinda seated at the table having her breakfast.

'Good morning, Bridget. Bring the money with you? I only bet on certainties.'

'Well, this time no one won. You'll have to wait and see. It was a draw or stalemate.' Bridget stood at the window watching Gareth and Jamie ride out, and all her joy in the day faded away. To think she had fought against going with them when she arrived, and now she was utterly miserable to miss out. What if the mysterious situation wasn't straightened out, and Gareth left tomorrow? She could not bear the thought.

Kathy came in with the children, still grizzling. 'Oh, I'm glad you're back, Bridget. Miss Curtis is having her breakfast in bed. She said you were to drive her to town and to be ready and waiting in an hour and a half. Can you drive that huge car?'

'Yes, but I'll have to be careful.'

'I can't even drive.' Kathy said regretfully.

Valinda laughed, 'You needn't worry about speed, driving Aunt Grace. She refuses to travel more than forty miles an hour. It's a bit like a ceremonial procession. Fancy her going up to town—must be something big. She usually summons anyone here to see her. This is a bit like the mountain going to Mahomet.'

'I'll have my breakfast, Kathy, and then take the kids off your hands for an hour,' said Bridget. 'I've got nothing else to do.'

'Would you? You're a darling! Matthew is getting

four teeth, and he's so scratchy, poor wee mite, and Kelly is matching him grizzle for grizzle.'

Valinda stood up, 'I wouldn't mind a day in town. I'll go and ask Aunt Grace if I can go with you.'

After she left the room, Kathy said, 'She's got Buckley's chance—Miss Curtis is in a fine fury, playing the grande dame to the full. Wouldn't the kids just pick today to play up? I'm glad she's going away for the day. What did Gareth say to you?'

'Just asked if I could drive the car, took me out for a trial run, and said to take good care of Miss Curtis.'

'Did he say anything about the quarrel?'

'Just that it would all work out.'

Kathy snorted, 'She's a damned fool if she lets him go. He's got a great reputation and she was lucky to get him as manager. It'll be no skin off his nose to leave here. He could walk into a better job any day. He's so patient with her and she frustrates most of his plans.'

Bridget gathered up Matthew and Kelly and went out into the garden to amuse them, finding a new lift in her step, a new song in her heart. So Gareth had not shared his ambitions with Kathy. Now she had a reason for her unreasonable happiness.

But the garden wasn't big enough for the children, and she gave in to Kelly's 'tows aden' plea. With Matthew on her back in a pack and Kelly's gracious invitation 'you may take my hand' accepted, she wandered off to where two large Hereford cows were grazing with their small, enchanting, doe-eyed calves near the men's quarters. Bridget kept behind the rickety fence, knowing that cows with calves could be very unpredictable. Then they visited the pond behind the stable where the geese and goslings swam, then back past the fowl run to feed the hens and collect the eggs.

'Tan I get the eggs, Bridget?' begged Kelly. 'I'll be very tareful. I'm big now. Matthew's only little.'

'All right, but we don't want scrambled eggs.'

Bridget kept her eye carefully on the little girl and, with eggs safely in the box, headed back to the house and deposited two much happier children with Kathy before going to her room to change. She was glad she had washed her hair and she swept the shining gold mass into a neat crown and pinned it securely, then put on her favourite apricot pleated dress and her high-heeled shoes. She only needed a light touch of make-up with her new tan, and eye-shadow and lipstick completed her preparations. She felt cool and summery, then she remembered the wind which often sprang up in the city and chose a cardigan.

She went along to Valinda's room. 'Are you going with us?' she asked.

'You'd be joking! With Aunt Grace in that mood I'm glad she said no. I need a few bits and pieces in town—here's a list. If you get the chance while she's at the lawyers I'd be pleased. Go to Whitcoull's and put them on Dad's account. And if you want a bit of free advice, don't speak until you're spoken to . . . that must have been one hell of a row last night. You look super in that outfit.'

'Thanks.' Bridget took the list and went downstairs with enough time in hand to share a cup of coffee with Kathy.

Kathy whistled when she saw her. 'You look a million dollars! What a pity the men aren't here to see you in all your glory, but I'll sure tell them what they missed. Seeing you all slender and willowlike convinces me I'll have to go back on my diet. You've lost weight since you've been here, and you didn't need to, and I've put it on. I'm so fat!'

Bridget smiled, 'You're not, you're just right. Anything you want in town, that's if I get the chance?'

'Thought you'd never ask,' Kathy giggled and handed over a list. 'I'd love a day in town myself, but I'll go on the bus. You'd better get out there.'

Bridget hastily swallowed her coffee and went through the hall just in time to meet Miss Curtis at the foot of the stairs.

'Good morning, Miss Curtis. I have the car waiting at the front door.'

Miss Curtis inclined her head slightly to show she had heard and proceeded down the hall with great dignity. Bridget was taken aback at her almost regal air and lofty reserve, then hurried forward to hold open the door. Again the slight nod of the elegant head. It was going to be a fun trip. She quickly moved past Miss Curtis on the front steps and opened the passenger door for her.

'I will sit in the back seat.'

'Certainly, Miss Curtis.' Bridget hastily opened the rear door, then closed it and took her place at the wheel somewhat shakily.

A sharp tap on her shoulder made her turn around. 'You're competent to drive?'

'Yes, Miss Curtis.'

'Then proceed.'

Bridget drove off feeling quite quelled. She felt she should have been wearing a chauffeur's uniform, and murmured 'Yes, ma'am, no ma'am.' Miss Curtis was usually so gentle and friendly, quite without formality. What a transformation! The big car purred along and as she gained confidence Bridget started to enjoy herself. She always loved driving.

It was a long trip at forty miles an hour, and every now and then she glanced in the rear vision mirror to check on Miss Curtis. Her expression never altered.

Bridget sighed. She was not going to get a chance to pour oil on troubled waters. She would leave it to the lawyers to put it in a diplomatic way, and if Miss Curtis needed her when it was over then she'd be as helpful as she could be. There was no use speculating on the outcome, her knowledge was too sketchy.

Another sharp tap on the shoulder gained her attention as she drove down the motorway.

'Take me to the Bridge of Remembrance on Cambridge Terrace.'

'Yes, mada ... Miss Curtis.' Bridget hoped like mad that she would find a parking meter free. Thank goodness the address was a well-known spot in Christchurch. Praise the Lord, there was room for the big car to park. She breathed a sigh of relief and hurried round to open the door for Miss Curtis.

'May I come with you?' she asked a trifle nervously.

'You may not. Be here at two o'clock sharp. I'm lunching with my solicitor and wish to do some shopping later.'

Bridget shrugged her shoulders helplessly as she watched the small determined figure walk erectly down the street and disappear into a doorway. She saw two passers-by turn and stare after Miss Curtis. No wonder, she looked so elegant in her soft lavender suit and snow-white blouse. and there were not many these days who wore immaculately matching hat, shoes and handbag, or carried themselves with such dignity.

Well, she couldn't just stand here, she would have to move the car or she'd end up with a parking ticket. She drove out to her flat and picked up a sheaf of letters from Andrew. Why wouldn't he stop writing? She drove back to the centre of town and put the car in a parking lot, then at her leisure did Valinda and Kathy's errands, and paid the large cheque Mr Mason had sent her into her bank. Six weeks' wages plus a little extra, he had written on a note enclosed. It was far too generous. Bridget read the note again. He said she must accept it, although there was no way money could parallel the gesture she had made. That was nice of him. She could indulge in a minor mad shopping spree. She bought gifts for her parents, books and toys for Matthew and Kelly, perfume for Kathy, and an exquisitely crafted heavy crystal paperweight for Valinda, then turned to her own needs. She bought some comfortable boots for riding, which was extravagant considering she hadn't much time left on the station. Next two pairs of slim-fitting cotton twill Levi jeans, one buttercream yellow, one lilac, an expensive intricately embroidered white linen shirt and a soft, flaring chamois wrap-around skirt.

The cost of the skirt steadied her instantly, and she bought a milk shake and sandwiches and carried them down to the green, sloping bank of the Avon River, away from the temptation of the shops. By the time she had eaten her lunch and read Andrew's letters, it was time to collect the car and drive back for Miss Curtis. She parked carefully sharp at two o'clock, then sat and waited. The minutes slipped slowly past and anxiety began to gnaw at her. What if Miss Curtis had had a heart attack? Or a stroke? Gareth would think her a pretty careless companion for not sticking around even though she had been told to leave. She didn't even know which solicitor in that building Miss Curtis was visiting. After half an hour she got out and put another coin in the meter, then went to stand at the doorway of the offices, and her heart lifted with relief as she saw Miss Curtis coming down the stairs on the arm of an elderly, white-haired gentleman.

Bridget went back to the car and stood ready with the back door open.

'I'll sit in the front with you, Bridget.' Miss Curtis's smile was a little wavery as if uncertain of her reception.

Bridget slammed the back door and opened the front one, 'I'm pleased to have your company.' She leaned over and adjusted the safety belt and clicked it shut, thankful to have Miss Curtis back safe and sound and in a friendly mood.

'You wanted to do some shopping, Miss Curtis?'

'No, thank you, dear, I've changed my mind. I just want to go home. I'm very tired.' She leaned back against the upholstery and closed her eyes.

Bridget concentrated on her driving until she was out of the city and moving along the motorway. She kept glancing over at the small silent figure and thought she was asleep, until she saw tears starting to slide down the wrinkled cheeks.

'Can I help you, Miss Curtis?' she asked. 'Would you like me to pull over and stop as soon as we're off the motorway?'

'No, no, don't stop. Just get me home. I've been a very foolish, arrogant woman, and I've brought myself to the brink of financial ruin. I wouldn't listen. Valinda's father, my dear nephew, tried to warn me, but I thought he was exaggerating. Now I have to face up to reality.'

Bridget felt a lump in her throat. She reached out with her free hand to touch and comfort Miss Curtis. 'I'm so very sorry. I really am.'

'I'm not deserving of your sympathy, or anyone else's. I said take me home, and it's not even my home any longer. It belongs to Gareth Evans. He's not the manager at all, he's the owner, and I've treated him so shabbily. Such a goodhearted young man! I've been shockingly rude to him, and made such difficulties for him over the property, and all the time I was living on his charity.'

'I don't believe it,' protested Bridget. 'How could it happen? You *must* be mistaken.'

'No, there's no mistake. I saw the papers today.'

'But wouldn't they have to get your consent to a sale? Wouldn't you have to sign something?' Bridget was appalled.

Miss Curtis shook her head. 'No. I'm not going into all the legal jargon, but it was held in trust for Valinda's father, although I had the right to control the affairs with advice from the land agents and solicitors during my lifetime. I wouldn't accept their advice. Even by the time father died the place was slipping badly, they told me. They hoped I would live out my life here and be none the wiser about the precarious money situation, and it would have happened that way except for my extravagance in doing up the house. You see, I didn't tell anyone I was planning to do that. I just called up an interior decorator and let him have a free hand. The cost was exorbitant. It drained away the last bit of equity in the Trust.'

'But they could have told you it was sold. It's a terrible shock for you to find out like this.'

'The blame is wholly and completely mine. As for telling me, they hoped I would never find out about the sale. Gareth would never have told me himself. He was actually prepared to leave if that was the only way to keep the secret. He rang the solicitors this morning, to that effect. And he didn't even mention it when I gave him his notice. How can I face him?'

Bridget didn't know how to answer. It was a mess. But how like Gareth it was, to make Miss Curtis still feel she was the owner. He would be more upset than she was to learn the lawyers had told her the truth. 'He loves you, Miss Curtis,' she said.

Miss Curtis straightened up and dabbed at her face with a dainty lace handkerchief. 'Not only him, there's Charles, my nephew. The station was to go to him. I had it only for my lifetime. *What* will he say?'

'He's been trying to advise you, Miss Curtis. He must know already how bad things are. If it had been really important to him he would have got through to you before this. Are either of his sons interested in Paradise Peaks?'

'No. It was a great disappointment to me. The land means nothing to them. Only Valinda has ever wanted to spend time here.' Miss Curtis gave a delicate sniff. 'That's not the point. I've wasted an inheritance through wilful extravagance. All the work my father and brothers and my uncles put in is lost because of me. I'm so ashamed, when I think of my grandfather and my great-grandfather. I could tell you of the hardships they faced, and all for nothing. I have nothing to show for a whole lifetime. I've been wanton and wasteful with something that was not my own.'

'That's not true,' Bridget protested. 'Look at the homestead, you've kept it beautifully. You can call that your tribute to the past. You've cheristed it, preserved it and cared for it, and the garden is all yours. You work so hard to keep it looking just right. You couldn't be expected to run a station of that size—that's man's work. You've done your share, Miss Curtis, really you have.'

'You're a very kind girl, Bridget, but it's no use. I stand condemned. I can't bear it, I can't endure it . . . When I think of the first men who took up the land . . . What would they say to me?'

All the fight had gone out of her, and Bridget ached with sympathy, but could think of nothing consoling to say. She had to get the old lady away from thinking of her own failure.

'Tell me how your people came here, Miss Curtis,' she asked, but the silence stretched and stretched. Desperately she asked, 'Have you any family records?'

'I have them all—diaries, photographs, going back over a hundred years. Such courage they had, especially the women. Roderick and Abigail Curtis arrived in Lyttleton with their family in 1850. They took a small cottage in Christchurch. They had four children and she was expecting a fifth. That baby was stillborn. They took up a small holding on the plains, but Roderick was not content. He rode far and wide, then he found Paradise Peaks, and he laid claim to it.' Miss Curtis sighed deeply. 'A heritage for his children, he called it.'

She was quiet again and Bridget concentrated on her driving, her eyes lifting to the foothills and the ranges beyond, and she felt a difference in the silence now, as if Miss Curtis was, like her, visioning the early settlers making their way towards the mountains.

Suddenly Miss Curtis brightened up and as if Bridget had touched the right chord in her memory she started to talk of the family, of the floods and fires and disasters, the excitement and joys and successes. The first house that was built, then the homestead, the planting of the trees and the woolclip and the wagons that carried them.

And as she spoke it all came alive to Bridget and she was surprised to find they were almost home.

'Oh, that's fantastic, Miss Curtis. Thank you for telling me. You know so much of the early history of this area as well as the story of your own family. Why don't you write it down? You say you have all the diaries. You could do it.'

'Who would be interested?'

'Me for one. And I'll guarantee your nephew, Mr Mason, would be delighted to have it written for him. So many stories have been lost as the generations have passed and few people would have your store of memories. Why not give that as your contribution to the past? That way the work that your family has done, their pioneering spirit, will live for always.'

'It would be a lot of work,' said Miss Curtis dubiously.

'For sure, but it would be worth it.' Bridget stopped at the turn off to pick up the milk crate and mail. When she got back in Miss Curtis was sitting forward on her seat with a bright, alert expression on her face.

'I'm going to do that—put it all down in sequence.'

I'm quite excited about it. Even if I have to leave here now I can take all my papers with me. I'll have something to do—a purpose, something worthwhile to leave behind.'

Bridget beamed at her. 'You certainly will! And I'll help you while I'm here. Valinda can too. She took typing as an option at school and if you get her interested I'm sure she'd rather be typing your notes than any other work. And Gareth won't let you leave, I promise you.'

'I won't accept charity. Why, he's not even family!'

As the car swept up to the front door and stopped, Miss Curtis smiled at Bridget. 'You're a good girl, Bridget. Thank you for coming with me today. The good Lord knew what he was doing when he sent you into this family.'

Bridget looked up to see Gareth coming down the front steps and muttered, 'I sure hope He did.'

'Good to see you home.' Gareth's smile was warm, but Bridget saw the concern in his eyes.

Miss Curtis allowed him to help her from the car, then said firmly, 'I'll speak to you in the library, young man.' She declined his arm and marched determinedly up the steps.

Gareth leaned over into the car. 'You've worked a miracle! No, don't shake your head at me. The lawyers rang as soon as she left and they described her condition; they reckoned she wouldn't see the week out. She'd given up, and yet you bring her back fighting fit. You have my sincere thanks.' He went to close the door, then poked his head in again. 'Who's Andrew?'

'Andrew?' Bridget repeated, dumbfounded.

'You said you used to drive Andrew's car. Is

he a brother? Friend?'

Bridget's eyes flashed. 'Andrew is none of your business!'

Gareth laughed. 'Ha! A friend? A special friend? Someone who hopes to marry you? Poor fellow. He's a born loser.'

He winked wickedly at her, then slammed the door and, seething, Bridget watched his lean, agile figure spring up the steps and disappear into the hall. She sat glaring after him, her heart in a tumult. She had been helping him, loving him, anxious for him, and so grateful that he was beginning to behave normally, and all he could do was tease and upset her. Imagine saying Andrew was a loser! Why, she would write and tell Andrew she'd marry him! No. She'd *ring* Andrew and tell him she'd marry him. That would show Gareth Evans where he got off!

She drove off, leaving a shower of gravel behind her, and put the car in the garage. Gathering up her parcels, she headed for the house, trying to control her temper, trying to think why she was so angry. Then it hit her. Gareth's teasing remark implied that Andrew was a loser because someone else wanted to marry her. Gareth himself! Flirting was one thing, but pretending he wanted to marry her was quite another. He was a monster!

Kathy's first question as Bridget walked into the kitchen was, 'Is it all right? Is Gareth staying?'

'Yes—*he'll* be staying,' and she piled all the parcels on the table, plucking out the perfume for Kathy. The rapturous welcome Kelly and Matthew gave her soothed her a little and their delight with the toys soon had her laughing. She was down on her hands and knees trying to fend Matthew and his new truck, 'brmm, brmm'ing away, off Kelly's carefully arranged blocks, when Gareth came in. Bridget did not see him for a few seconds as Matthew, with the strength of a small bulldozer, had his arms around her neck and was trying to remove her from his path by force.

'Oh, Matthew!' she protested as he loosened the pins from her hair and it came tumbling down about her shoulders, much to his delight.

'When they can spare you, Miss Curtis would like a word with you. Put the kettle on, please, Kathy. We won't be long and a cuppa would go down well.'

Bridget looked up, her face flushed and her hair dishevelled, and still mirrored in her green-gold eyes, the fun she'd been enjoying. 'I'll go and do my hair, and be right in,' she said.

'You look absolutely beautiful. You'll be fine as you are.' Gareth bent down and lifted her to her feet. She looked at him, trying to reach back for the feeling of anger, but it was gone, and only the years of loving were left. She bit her lip and walked ahead of him through the hall.

At the foot of the stairs, he stopped her. 'Bridget.'

'Yes?' She did not turn around.

'Look at me.'

She swung around, her eyes bright with unshed tears, but her small chin lifted defiantly, fighting with every fibre of her being to conceal from him the intensity of the love she felt for him. How could the mere touch of his hand and a careless compliment arouse such a floodtide of emotion within her?

His brown eyes travelled over her as warm as a caress, from the tip of her head to the swirling golden mass of her hair settling about her shoulders, down over her body outlined in the brilliant sunshine pouring through the front door, to her long slender legs and elegant high-heeled shoes, then back to her eyes.

He shook his head. 'No, it's gone. For a moment there I thought I remembered who you were. It was so close, so real ... When you were sitting there with the kids. You were very young when I knew you, Bridget. Is that true?'

Bridget's breath clotted in her throat, she found it difficult to speak. 'Yes, I was very young, naïve and stupid.' She pushed herself away from the stair balustrade and walked into the library.

Miss Curtis was sitting by the window. She patted the chair beside her. 'Come and sit by me, Bridget. Gareth, do sit down instead of towering over us like that.'

He sat down opposite, stretching out his long legs comfortably, his eyes narrowed a little against the sun, but still watching Bridget intently. 'Angel and I have been letting the dust settle a little and we've come to an agreement,' he said. 'For the present things are going to continue exactly as they've always been. Only we three will know the true situation. Do you understand?'

'Yes,' Bridget nodded, wondering how he had got Miss Curtis to agree, then not wondering. When Gareth put his mind to anything he could charm the birds out of the trees.

Miss Curtis leaned forward, her face flushed and excited. 'Of course, I didn't let him off lightly for deceiving me, but when he explained the family connection I could understand why he had done it. It means so very much to me, almost a miracle. And he wants me to write the family history too. I must admit that the thought of leaving here was tearing me in two. Who could believe that a day that started off so badly could finish so well? I think we'll have a sherry to celebrate. Gareth?'

A broad smile creased his attractive face. 'Who indeed? I'll get the drinks.'

Resentfully Bridget watched his lean sinewy figure disappear. Did anything ever turn out wrong for him? It wasn't fair that any man could have so much intelligence and charm and be lucky too!

'Isn't he wonderful?' Miss Curtis was looking after him fondly. 'My father would have admired him so much. It seems wrong not to announce that he now owns Paradise Peaks, but he said for business reasons it was better for me to be seen as I always was— gave a sense of stability in the district as well. Even though he explained it I couldn't quite grasp what he meant. Do you understand?'

'Oh, yes, I understand,' Bridget said warmly, her resentment easing away. Gareth was doing it because he knew how hard it would be for Miss Curtis to be deposed—and yes, she loved him for it.

He came back with a crystal decanter and three glasses and poured a generous measure for each of them. 'The toast will be to Paradise Peaks and health, happiness and prosperity to all who work here.'

The glasses touched and the toast was drunk. Miss Curtis said, 'This is one of the happiest days of my whole life. I feel the station has taken on a new lease of life since you came here, Gareth. I always had my garden and the house, but I was so lonely. But when you made me come out and share my meals with you and the men, and Kathy and the children, you gave me new friends. It's very interesting and stimulating. I thank you for that. And I have much to thank you for too, Bridget, for your kindness today, and daily I see your love and influence changing

Valinda's attitude. Your example and encouragement are making her search out new values for her
life, so that I can really believe the court will approve
her probation. You're both my very dear friends.'

'And you're very dear to us too, Angel.' Gareth
leaned forward and kissed her. 'That's allowed, you
know. I'm almost family.'

'You *are* family,' Miss Curtis corrected him. 'I
would never agree to this arrangement had that not
been so. May I tell that to the others? It's too good
to keep to myself.'

Gareth laughed, 'Certainly, if it pleases you.'

'Let's go and tell Kathy now.' She hurried ahead
of them from the room.

'It's been a great day for me as well,' Gareth
smiled down at Bridget. 'Has it been good for you
too?'

Bridget stood up and gave him a level glance.
'Like the curate's egg—good in parts.'

'We'll be tailing tomorrow, but I want to have a
quick look how the feed is holding, down on Eden
Block—you know, behind Peter, Paul and Luke.
There's enough light in the evenings now, so I'll ride
out there after dinner. Would you like to come with
me?'

'I would not.'

His grin broadened, and the mocking laughter was
back in his eyes. 'Discretion being the better part of
valour?'

For once her composure did not crack under his
teasing and she tilted her face and laughed up at
him, 'He who fights and runs away, lives to fight
another day.' She moved quickly towards the door.
It was no use pushing her luck. Oh, wouldn't it be
wonderful if she could always hold her own with

Gareth? If only she could control her emotions all the time! If only she didn't care so much . . .

At the dinner table, Gareth asked Doug, 'How long before the new paddock will be ready for sowing?'

'A week, ten days. It's a big area, Gareth, and you want it just spot on. What's the weather report like?'

'That's what I'm thinking of. The long-range forecast is for rain after the weekend. I'd like to whip it in before that to have some good fattening feed after Christmas. We'll do a twenty-four-hour shift on it, I think. I'll take over when you knock off. We'd make it by Friday, do you think?'

'Should do.' Doug was always a man of few words.

Kathy called, 'You're wanted on the phone, Gareth.'

When he came back he was looking pleased. 'Well, that's settled. We make a try for the wild cattle the weekend after next. That was Morgan Grant from Evangeline, he's got a couple of chaps there who want to have a go, and says there's three of your rodeo mates at Hopefield, Jamie. He said he'd probably come with us, Tay as well. But he wants us to go there for a barbecue this Saturday night and we'll discuss it then. You're all invited.'

'Whoopee! That's great,' exclaimed Jamie. 'Did he say who was at Hopefield? No backing out of this night, Bridget. You'll enjoy yourself, that's a promise. I'll ride out with you tonight, Gareth, and we'll bring a few spare horses in. They'll need a bit of education, running wild for so long, and we'll have to be able to rely on them with those cattle.'

'You'll all go to the barbecue,' Miss Curtis said

firmly. 'I'll babysit the wee ones.'

'Oh, no,' Bridget protested, 'I will. Matthew is too heavy for you to lift out of the cot.'

'Nonsense! Kathy can settle them down for the night. It won't matter if she's a little late arriving.'

Doug looked up. 'I'll wait back for you, Kathy.'

'That's settled,' said Gareth with much satisfaction, flicking a wicked glance at Bridget as if he knew how much she was trying to squirm out of going.

Would her emotions always be in conflict? Half of her longed to go to the barbecue, to laugh and talk, perhaps to dance with Gareth in a new setting, the other part warned her of the danger of doing just that. It was the same about staying at Paradise Peaks, one part of her wanted the visit to be over, to get away from the tension and strain of being constantly in Gareth's company, the other part warned of the long, dull empty days ahead, never seeing him again, only warmed by memories.

Matthew caused a slight distraction by emptying his meal on to his high-chair tray and finger-painting in the goo, pushing the extra over the side on to the floor.

'Matthew! You *dear* little thing!' His mother swooped on him with a damp cloth, completely destroying his artistic efforts and his fun. There ensued the usual struggle while he was made suitable for public viewing again and he was released for the after tea games of chase and push with Kelly. They'd run madly around, then he's stand and wait for her to push him over. It was none too gentle, but he greeted every fall with giggles and came round for more.

After the children were put down and the dishes done the three girls joined Miss Curtis in the library.

Valinda and Kathy were delighted with the news that a story of the station was to be written, and wanted to help sort out the material.

'I can do with all your enthusiasm and energy,' Miss Curtis told them. 'I think it would be best if we sorted all the material into chronological order, starting from their arrival on the boat. Oh, this is really exciting!'

Not much work was done the first night because each photograph and letter brought back so many memories, but Bridget felt that T.V. was going to be very short of viewers for some time. Valinda rushed upstairs and brought down her tape recorder and showed her aunt how to work it. They were still deeply engrossed when Gareth came back and complained because Kathy couldn't tear herself away to make supper. He became fascinated by the early farm diaries, and it was quite late before they all made their way up to bed.

Bridget's second last thought before she fell asleep was that she would be leaving before the project really got under way. She wanted to be part of it all. Her last thought was that, with any luck, she might break a leg before the barbecue so that the decision would be taken out of her hands.

CHAPTER EIGHT

THE week before the barbecue raced away, and the pressure of work kept Gareth from tormenting Bridget very much. He drove the tractor through till daybreak each morning, showered and changed and ate his breakfast with the rest, then put in a day mustering and tailing the lambs with such drive that it left Bridget completely exhausted by night time. Far from looking worn out with lack of sleep, he seemed to thrive on it.

Nothing intervened to prevent Bridget from going. She glared balefully at her well-shaped legs in the mirror as she dressed. Even a sprained ankle would have been enough excuse, and she did not have as much as a stubbed toe.

She checked in the mirror, admiring her trim figure-hugging new Levis and utterly feminine embroidered shirt. She was glad she had spent so extravagantly. If she had to go, she wanted to look her best. Her hair was neatly plaited and wound in an attractive coronet, the style emphasising her slender neck and the soft contours of her face.

'I'll stay well clear of Gareth Evans tonight, she told herself. It should be easy, there'll be a lot of people there.'

The admiration in Gareth's eyes was a little unnerving and she was glad when Jamie came in and whistled loudly. 'Bridget, you look fabulous! You have to travel with me in the 'ute, you wouldn't be safe with anyone else.'

'And I'll be safe with you?' Bridget asked with a laugh.

'We'll find out. That should make the evening interesting.'

'You'll bring Valinda, Gareth?'

'Have I any choice?' He seemed quite un-perturbed.

' 'Fraid not. I spoke first. It might be good for the country to conserve fuel and all travel together, but it's death on romance. Anyway, I like having my own set of wheels. Do you want us to take any of that food, Kathy?'

'No, I'll give it to Gareth and Valinda when she comes down. I haven't quite finished decorating the pavlovas yet.'

Jamie nodded, 'Right, we're on our way.' He caught Bridget's hand and ran her down the path.

Bridget enjoyed the drive and Jamie's nonsense. He was fun to be with, and she knew he liked her. His flirting and his casual compliments were light-hearted and amused her. When Gareth did exactly the same thing she either got uptight or acted like a spineless jellyfish. But the night had started off well, and she wouldn't spoil it by thinking of Gareth.

'You'll enjoy this lot,' Jamie remarked as he swung off the main road and headed towards a plateau with buildings and houses all about it like a small village. 'Morgan got married about a year ago to a darling-looking girl from Scotland. Her name is Katriona. She's redheaded and has taken to high-country life like a duck to water. Then there's Tay and Amber, his wife. He's the head shepherd. It's a well-run place, a happy station, but they've done away with the horses, so it wouldn't suit me. Here's the new house.'

He led Bridget in and introduced her all round, before taking her to sit beside the swimming pool by his three mates.

'What will you have to drink, Bridget?' he asked.

'Something nice and cool.'

'Right. And you lot may look, but that's all. She's my girl!'

He walked away to the jeering calls of, 'She's got no taste,' and 'She needs rescuing immediately!'

Bridget liked them and when Jamie came back was surprised how easily they accepted her. Then Gareth came in with Valinda and just the sight of him set her pulses racing, much to her dismay. Valinda joined them, but Bridget was thankful to see Gareth move over to where Tay and Morgan Grant were seated with their wives on another terrace.

Kathy and Doug arrived and joined them. Kathy's sweet face was lit with a new beauty and her eyes turned often to Doug, soft and wondering and loving. When she got a chance she slipped into a place beside Bridget.

'I've got to talk to someone or I'll bust! Doug has asked me to marry him. I can't believe it!'

'Oh, Kathy, that's fantastic! Did you say yes?'

Kathy shook her head. 'He wouldn't let me. He said he just wanted me to know how he felt towards me and give me time to think about it. You know how he loves the kids, they think he's the greatest. Oh, Bridget, tell me what to do!'

Bridget laughed, 'I don't think I have to, you're lit up like a Christmas tree. I'm so happy for you. Didn't you have any idea?'

'Well, not really. Before you came here he always used to hang back after dinner and help me with the kids and the clearing up, and share my cuppa, and we talked a lot.'

'He must have loved me appearing on the scene,' Bridget said ruefully.

'Oh, don't think that. He likes you, and he knew it was good for me to have a friend like you—he said so. And we did have fun at the pub that night. I couldn't have gone if you hadn't been there. He's such a shy man, yet quiet and strong. Oh, I'm tempted ... I've been so lonely. That's no reason for getting married. I've been married and I was never more lonely in my life. I got married then for all the wrong reasons and as it got worse, I just kept thinking we needed more time. That wasn't true. Brent was playing the field. He was getting ready to leave me when he was killed. I haven't told anyone this, not even my family. It hurt so much. He didn't even *like* Kelly, just thought she was a nuisance.'

'I'm so sorry, Kathy,' Bridget said sympathetically. 'I won't tell anyone.'

'I know you won't. You're like Doug in that. I can talk about anything to him and not feel ashamed or stupid. He sort of makes me feel worthwhile. The way you do ... it's beaut.' Her eyes brimmed with tears. 'Oh, Bridget, what shall I do? I swore after Brent's funeral that I'd never marry again. I got hurt too much. Yet I do long for love and security, for all the things that go with a good marriage.'

Bridget put her arm around her. 'I think Doug must understand that. He hasn't pressured you. Take your time, get to know him, find out if you can trust him. There's no hurry, Kathy.'

'But I *do* trust him, already. That Sunday you went out to the wilderness he took the kids and me for a picnic, and although he didn't say or do anything special, I felt sort of protected and warm. I love him for even asking me the way he did, sort of quiet and sure and confident. Yet I know how terribly shy he is. It must have taken raw courage to ask me and risk rejection. I think it's beaut!'

'I think it's beaut too, Kathy,' smiled Bridget. 'I think there's happiness ahead for you, and for Kelly and Matthew. He's looking over here now. I think you'd better get back, or he'll know you've been talking about it to me.'

Kathy stood up, and straightened her pretty, flaring red skirt. 'He'll know anyway. But he won't mind, not if it's you. I told you, he likes you. Thanks for listening. You've helped me a lot—but I knew you would.'

Bridget tried to think back on what she had said that had helped Kathy, and couldn't find anything of value. The music had started and she watched Doug and Kathy go to join the dancers on the flat patio by the house. Even the way they moved together was beautiful to watch. Kathy already knew her answer—she just wanted to talk it over. Lucky Kathy!

'Will you eat first, or dance?' Jamie was pulling her to her feet.

'You choose.'

'Those steaks smell too good to wait. Come on!'

Bridget searched the crowd for Gareth. He wasn't anywhere near her. She had intended avoiding him, so why was she so disappointed and hurt when he was doing exactly what she had wanted? Suddenly she saw him dancing with a small dark girl. Bridget remembered Jamie introducing her as Amber, the head shepherd's wife. Well, she didn't have to worry whether they were enjoying themselves, they were giving it all they had, and Amber's enchanting face and green witch-eyes were showing, expressively, her joy.

Just then the music stopped and, as if Gareth had been aware of her scrutiny, he turned and looked straight at her with that tender, mocking expression which made her go weak at the knees. She turned away, and gave her attention to the succulent steaks sizzling on the grill. 'Mushrooms, Jamie!'

'Here's the plate, go and put some bread and salad on and then we get our steaks and mushrooms. Look at the spread! And if you've got any space left later that table over there is groaning with pavs, trifles, and cakes galore. Enjoying yourself?'

'Tremendously!' And it was true. There was a happy, relaxed atmosphere of people who knew and understood each other, and it was a beautiful setting. Everyone had arrived with happy, expectant faces and with the sole object of enjoying themselves, and they were doing it. Children ran in and out excitedly.

'Kathy could have brought Kelly, she would have loved it,' Bridget remarked as they made their way back to the group which had increased in size.

'Yes, I know,' Jamie replied. 'But Miss Curtis seemed to really get a kick out of being trusted with them.'

As the evening wore on Jamie turned his attention to more serious drinking, but Bridget did not lack for partners. Each time she joined the dancers Gareth was dancing with a different girl, although he danced with Valinda three times. Bridget felt humiliated that she even kept count, but she couldn't help it. She laughed, she sang and she danced, but the fact that Gareth was completely ignoring her left a huge aching emptiness in her that grew and grew until it became almost unbearable. She longed to go home, to go somewhere alone where she could cry it all out.

When the first couples started to leave she joined Jamie's group again and attempted to find out when they would be going home.

'We'll be here to the bitter end, Bridget. We'll make a night of it. Here, sit down and have another drink.'

Bridget accepted a glass and listened to them reliving their greater rodeo triumphs, but she was getting tired and wanted to get the evening over. Suddenly she remembered Kathy saying that they'd be leaving early and she went in search of her, only to find that Doug and Kathy had already gone, and so had many others. The crowd had thinned remarkably.

She started looking for Valinda and was standing under a slender birch tree at the edge of the lights when Gareth spoke. 'My dance, I think.'

Wordlessly she followed him towards the music. He was diabolically clever, but she could have no more refused him than flown to the moon. He spoke to the couple at the stereo and seconds later the fast, loud beat of the music died and the sweet, poignant strains of a waltz took their place. Again Bridget felt the same feeling of two rivers joining and flowing together. The lights dimmed one by one and she melted against him, matching his steps as if she had been born for this one dance. Like a butterfly that sheds its chrysalis and lives for a day, she would give herself to this one moment of bliss.

Gareth's arms drew her closer yet and she felt his lips against her hair, then his cheek against hers, and smelt the spicy, clean scent of his aftershave.

Then his lips against her ear, 'I've been waiting all night for this dance.'

Bridget wanted to be angry at him. His timing had been so exquisitely perfect, it was almost like being the victim of psychological warfare, but it was so sweet losing that she could not protest. Oh, that the music would go on for ever, and the fluid magic matching of their steps would never stop!

But the music did stop, and she found herself in a laughing, happy group of Gareth's friends, Morgan and his beautiful redheaded wife Katriona, Tay and the green-eyed Amber.

Katriona caught her arm. 'I've been meaning to get hold of you all night, but being hostess I've been too involved. Now it's over, you and Gareth must come and have coffee with us. Part of the fun of a party is holding the post-mortem afterwards.'

Bridget, with Gareth's arm about her, followed unresistingly in their wake, and for the next hour enjoyed herself more than she had the whole time of the barbecue. In the warmth of acceptance of her she relaxed and her personality expanded so that she was soon trading laughing insults and banter as if she'd known these people all her life.

As they said goodbye at the door, Katriona insisted, 'You come down and visit us again—that's an order. You haven't met my father yet, or my brand new daughter. You bring her Gareth.'

'It's a promise, Katriona. I'll give you a ring.'

They were standing by the car before Bridget realised it, and protested, 'I didn't come with you. Where's Valinda?'

'Oh, she took off with an extremely eligible young man of impeccable background, who she said she rather fancied. She asked my permission, and as he's a pleasant but harmless youth, in spite of her calling him the Hottest Breath in the West, I gave it to her.'

'Why didn't she ask me?' Bridget demanded indignantly.

'Because you might have said no, because you might have decided to chaperon them.'

'And Jamie?' But she already knew the answer. He had it all worked out that she was going to be taken home by himself.

'Jamie is in no condition to drive you home. I sent him off home while you were helping the girls prepare the coffee. His mates went with him, they're staying in the men's quarters tonight and going to take a look-see at the wilderness tomorrow, if their heads can stand it.'

'You knew when Jamie wanted to bring me here tonight that he'd get drunk, didn't you?' she accused.

Gareth laughed. 'Of course I knew. He always does. Why do you think I didn't protest?' He opened the car door. 'I'm taking you home.'

'Have I any choice?'

'None whatever,' he said with immense satisfaction. 'Hop in.' Bridget did, and watched him stride around the front of the car, and she inched nearer the door when he sat in the driver's seat.

He smiled as he drove off, but once out on the main road, he patted the seat near him. 'Move a bit closer, Bridget, come and keep me warm.'

'No. I don't care if you freeze to death.'

'That's very harsh,' he complained. 'I just want to talk to you. I'm a very nice polite young man, I work hard, have good prospects and my intentions are very honorable.'

Bridget heard the laughter in his voice. 'I dislike

people who do their own commercials, they always reek of insincerity.'

He chuckled. 'There's another way of doing this, which isn't at all polite, but I'll use if it you continue to keep your distance from me as if I had some communicable disease. You're alone with me on an isolated country road, and I'm much bigger than you are, much stronger and much more determined than you would ever believe. Now move over or I'll stop this car and drag you over.'

Bridget glared at him. 'You would, too!'

'Try me.'

She bit her lip and moved a little towards the centre.

'Closer.' As she inched another fraction nearer him, his left arm came off the steering wheel and pulled her close. 'There, that's much more friendly. If you relaxed your head on my shoulder it would be more comfortable for you. But if you perfer to sit awkwardly you'll end up with a crick in your neck.'

'You're speaking from years of experience of molesting girls, I presume?' she asked furiously.

'That's right,' he answered pleasantly.

As the miles slipped by, the truth of his remark manifested itself and she felt cramp attack her rigid body and had to move to ease it. The warmth of the car and the immeasurable comfort of his arm about her and her own weariness defeated her, and her head rested lightly against his shoulder.

'You remind me of a girl I knew years ago,' Gareth told her. 'She wasn't at all like you physically, except perhaps about the eyes. She was a darling. We spent a lot of time together, and I think I was closer to her than any other girl I've ever met. She had the same direct honesty you have, the same gutsy courage.

She had intelligence too, and had a capacity to give out love that I've never seen equalled.'

'What was her name?' Bridget couldn't help herself.

'Bonnie. She was a right character. I liked her the moment I set eyes on her, but she was so shy and quiet, it took me ages to draw her out. When I did it was well worth the effort. That kid had something very special. The more layers you unwrapped the more depth of character you found, and you knew you could know her for a lifetime and she'd always come up with something fresh and exciting. Life would never have grown stale or samey with her.'

Bridget pressed her lips together and tried to control her breathing, so Gareth wouldn't guess she was so shaken. 'She sounds like the one with your name written on her. Why didn't you marry her?'

'Hell, I couldn't do that. She was only a little kid. I never thought of her like that. We were just friends. Anyway, I had this sort of understanding with Liz. We'd grown up together, wrote to each other, and when she came down to visit, she expected us to announce our engagement. Sounds a bit wishy-washy, but it's harder to dodge out of an obligation like that than you'd believe, so we announced it and got it over.'

'But you didn't marry her?'

'No. It was supposed to be a long-term thing, we weren't in a hurry. I think she just liked the idea of getting engaged. I mean, we liked each other and I thought we'd go well together, the same interests, same backgrounds. I thought, if I thought at all, that we'd grow closer to each other, but the reverse happened. As time went on we had less and less in common, and I knew there was no way I could spend the rest of my life with her.'

'So what did you do?'

'Sat it out, until she got so impatient with me that she started going out with someone else. She really fell in love with Jim, and gave my ring back. It was a close shave.'

'You sound like a bad risk to me. Real bachelor material,' Bridget said hastily.

'You're wrong there. I intend to get married. I know what I'm looking for now. Young Bonnie taught me that. I've been watching a lot of marriages, trying to see why some hang together and others split up. Physical attraction isn't enough, common interests aren't enough, although they help; there also has to be friendship, a deep, loyal, abiding joy in each other's company. Like Morgan and Katriona have ... and Tay and Amber. Bonnie showed me that two people could be bonded together in true friendship without sex coming into it at all. So I've been searching for a girl who could give me that. It's impossible to define, but she set me a standard that I knew I had to have before I'd consider sharing my life with anyone.'

He braked the car, and switched off the engine. 'We're home, Bridget.'

He had moved his arm from around her to switch off the car and she moved like lightning to fling open the door and escape. She couldn't let him see her crying. She ran towards the house, but Gareth caught her before she reached the back gate and turned her round to face him.

'Why, Bridget, you're crying!' He was shocked. 'Did I say anything to make you cry?'

She gulped and tried to wipe the tears that wouldn't stop. He cradled her in his arms. 'Tell me why you're crying?'

'For Bonnie. For that poor kid who must have loved you, and you just let her walk out of your life.' She sniffed and hiccoughed, both together. 'You're a brute! You took all that girl had to offer and then your old playmate arrived and you just flipped her to one side. How old was she?'

'Here, wait a minute! I wasn't like that,' Gareth protested. 'She was only seventeen, still at school. It was friendship, nothing more. You're making too much of it, getting upset for nothing.'

'I am not!' Bridget shouted wildly. 'She was as old as Valinda. Do you think Valinda is too young to know if she met real love?'

'No, I don't . . . but Bonnie wasn't like that at all. She was a sweet, loving kid . . .'

'And sex didn't come into it. You never kissed her, not once?' Bridget cried.

'Well, yes, I did, once . . . no, twice,' he admitted. 'Look, it was nearly four years ago.'

'Yet it still lingers in your memory. It must have devastated her.'

'There's only one way to stop you talking,' Gareth muttered angrily, and his mouth came down on hers with a fierce passion that bruised her lips, and she struggled against him until, within seconds, her hidden love welled up in response to his demand and overwhelmed her resistance.

At last he lifted his lips from hers and looked deep into her eyes. 'Ah, Bridget, Bridget . . .'

The she became aware that all the outside lights had come on, bathing them in brightness, and Valinda was running towards them with two five-dollar notes in her hand, and behind her, laughing, were Jamie and his friends.

'Well done, Gareth!' Valinda laughed. Turning to Bridget, she said, 'I tried to stir him into some action at the barbecue, to dance with you. When he wouldn't, I said he was scared and bet him he couldn't kiss you.'

'As if I didn't know that!' Bridget forced what she hoped was a natural laugh, and took the notes. 'One for you, Gareth, and one for me. We planned it together to teach you to stop taking bets all the time. You're the loser, Valinda.'

She never looked at Gareth or she would have seen the stunned look in his eyes. 'Goodnight, Gareth, thanks for your co-operation.' She stopped by the group of men and, if her smile was over-bright, they weren't in any condition to notice. 'Had a good party, Jamie?'

'Sure did. Great night. That was a good trick you pulled on Valinda.'

'It was indeed. That's the second bet she's lost to me. Should cure her, don't you think? See you in the morning.'

She heard their chorus of goodnights as she made it through to the kitchen, but once inside she ran across the room and up the stairs and shut her bed-room door, then flung herself on top of the bed and let the tears flow.

She heard someone knock on her door but ignored it. It seemed hours later when she pulled herself to-gether and bathed her face, and unwound her hair. Sitting in her robe, she automatically counted the strokes as she brushed her hair. She felt nothing now, not the pain or humiliation of knowing it was just a trick, or not even any compassion for the poor stupid

Bonnie. She was empty, drained of all emotion.

She walked over to the dresser to put the brush down, and heard a light knock on the door. She hesitated and looked at her watch. It was almost morning. She walked to the door.

'Who is it?'

'Gareth. Can I speak to you? I saw your light was still on.'

'You can go to . . . you can get lost!'

'Look, I want to apologise for that scene down there. I was as surprised as you were. Valinda was fooling around at the party, kidding me, and yes, she did make that bet, but I didn't take her up on it. I thought she was just fooling. I never thought about it again. You've got to believe me.'

'Pigs might fly,' Bridget answered rudely.

'Come on out. Come down to the kitchen and have some coffee with me. I've got something to say to you that I can't say through a closed door.'

'I've got nothing to say to you.' She leaned against the door, feeling too weak to stand up. 'If you don't go away immediately I'm going to scream this house down. I'm going to scream rape, and rip my night-dress, and see how you talk your way out of that one.'

'That I've got to see.' Gareth was laughing again. 'You sure don't know when to quit fighting, do you? I kissed you because I like kissing you. In fact to say I like kissing you is the biggest under-statement of the year. Bridget Marlow, I love you.'

'You'll be the laughing stock of the district,' she threatened, but crazy as it was, she was starting to believe him.

'Didn't you hear me? I said I love you. If you'd

open this door just an inch I'll propose to you. You'd better hurry up, or you might miss the chance of a lifetime. This offer may *not* be repeated.'

Bridget giggled. He loved her. He wanted to marry her. And he *had* loved Bonnie. She could forgive him anything, because he had truly loved that freaky fat funny girl who had been her so long ago. Suddenly her heart was singing a new song, a song that soared and soared higher than her beloved amethyst hills. Gareth loved her!

Then she heard him speak out loud, 'Only me, Angel. No, there's nothing wrong. I'm just proposing to Bridget and she's thinking it over. Go back to bed. You can congratulate us in the morning.'

'I look awful!' Bridget wailed.

'Not to me,' Gareth assured her. 'You're always beautiful to me, you always will be. Now open the door so I can propose properly. Do you want to tell our children that you accepted me from behind two inches of wood?'

'Our children,' she repeated on a sigh. Slowly she turned the door knob and stepped into his arms.

After a long, satisfying silence Gareth spoke. 'I'm not going to ask you to marry me here. We're going to ride out to the foot of Peter, Paul and Luke, and tie our horses to a tree by the creek and then climb to the top. We'll sit there quietly until the sun rises, and there you'll promise to be my wife. I'm a romantic at heart, but don't you tell anyone.'

Bridget laughed, 'I don't need to, it shows.'

He buried his face in her hair. 'Don't plait your hair, Bridget, not this morning.'

'I won't,' she promised. 'Now let me go and I'll get dressed while you catch the horses.'

His smile held a rare tenderness. 'They're already caught and saddled.'

'You were so sure?' Her voice was soft with wonder.

'Absolutely sure, from the first moment I set eyes on you. Now hurry, you have exactly five minutes to dress. My timing is perfect. I've been sitting in the kitchen this past hour, waiting to come to you, and we'll be there at the exact moment the dawn is breaking.'

'What if I'd been asleep?' she asked.

'I would have woken you up. What if you'd resisted? I wouldn't have let you. I would have plucked you from your bed and carried you in front of my saddle to the mountain top.'

'In my nightie?' Bridget tried to look shocked, but failed because she could not help smiling.

'In your nothing, if necessary. I knew you belonged to me. I was just giving you a bit of leeway, but enough is enough. Now dress.' Gareth pushed her through the door, as if knowing she could not leave him of her own strength.

She flung herself into the first clothes she saw, the lilac trousers and embroidered shirt, thrust her stockinged feet into her new riding boots, and washed her face, then brushed her wheaten-gold hair with long firm strokes and caught it back from her face with a small headscarf. She stared into the mirror, at the starry-eyed girl with the softly curving mouth. Then she ran down the stairs and out to the stable where Gareth was holding the horses, and Joe rushed barking to meet her like a demented monster.

'Get right on Nadia, and don't look at me like that or we'll never leave the homestead,' Gareth said firmly.

He held his big gelding in a little as they galloped down the lightening tussock plain, so that Nadia could indulge in her annoying habit of not being content unless she got her head first in any race, and it gave him a better view of his slender companion as she rode with her golden hair streaming out behind her like a banner.

Bridget pulled Nadia back into line just before they reached the creek and offered breathlessly, as she dismounted, 'It would look a bit too eager if I beat you to the top.'

'No chance. Save your breath.' He caught her hand and started to climb. 'I've been toughening you up for this climb ever since you arrived!'

Bridget did not answer, and felt the twenty-minute climb nearly killed her. Up and up and up, and all around them the tussocks swayed and moved as the wind sang its glorious song. Once she thought she would die if he didn't stop and give her a rest, then she got her second wind and the last hundred yards seemed effortless.

A sheltered rocky outcrop gave them a perfect view of her wonderful amethyst hills and beyond them range after range, already silhouetting against the pink flare of the breaking dawn.

'We'll wait until the first tip of the sun appears,' Gareth said quietly.

Nestled in his arms Bridget, knew she had to speak. 'Gareth, I've got to tell you something.'

'Nothing you can tell me now will change my mind, or my love for you.'

'I'm Bonnie.' It came out baldly, like a badly timed confession, and she hid her face in his chest.

Gently he tilted her face towards him just as the sun burst forth in a crimson blaze. 'I knew that I'd always known you, that I had always loved you. Bridget—Bonnie Marlow, will you marry me?'

'Yes, oh, yes!' Her voice was soft, and the glory that Jody had predicted shone in her face.

Mills & Boon
Best Seller Romances

The very best of Mills & Boon Romances
brought back for those of you who missed
them when they were first published.

In September
we bring back the following four
great romantic titles.

ETERNAL SUMMER
by Anne Hampson

Greece, the land of the ancient gods and of eternal summer;
all its beauty spots — Delphi, Athens, the glittering islands; all
these were to be part of Marika's daily life — if she agreed to
Nickolas Loukas's strange proposal. But would the price be
too high?

THE TOWER OF THE WINDS
by Elizabeth Hunter

When her sister died, Charity was determined to take care of
her baby son — but the child's uncle, the masterful Greek
Loukos Papandreous, was equally determined that the baby
was going to remain in Greece — with him. How could
Charity cope with this man who insisted that, as she was a
woman, her opinions were of no account — yet who made
her more and more glad she was a woman?

MAN IN A MILLION
by Roberta Leigh

Harriet wrote a best-seller and was given the chance of pro-
ducing it as a million-dollar movie. But Joel Blake, the owner
of the studio, believed that women were unfitted for such
work and made his opinion plain. Did it really matter to
Harriet what he thought? As time went by it appeared that it
did?

TENDER IS THE TYRANT
by Violet Winspear

'I — I sensed something *ruthless* about him. He moulds
people to his tastes, and he makes them submit whether they
want to or not,'Lauri described Maxim di Corte to her aunt
Pat when, as an inexperienced girl, Lauri first joined Maxim's
famous ballet company. There was no doubt that Maxim di
Corte would use these ruthless qualities to make her submit
to him as a dancer, but could he make her do the same for
him — as a woman?

If you have difficulty in obtaining any of these books through
your local paperback retailer, write to:

Mills & Boon Reader Service
P.O. Box 236, Thornton Road, Croydon, Surrey, CR9 3RU.